ISLEWORTH MADONNA

FICTION FROM TIGER OF THE STRIPE

*The Mischief-Maker
or the Loathsome History of a Malcontent*
JULIA LACEY BROOKE

Circled by the Sands
JULIA LACEY BROOKE

Afghan Silk
JULIA SCOTT

ISLEWORTH MADONNA

A PROFESSOR GERRISH GRAY MYSTERY

ANTON DE MORESCO

*McGonagall Professor of Experimental Prosody
at the University of Isleworth*

RICHMOND · TIGER OF THE STRIPE
MMXVI

First published in 2016 by
TIGER OF THE STRIPE
50 Albert Road
Richmond
Surrey TW10 6DP
United Kingdom

Revised June 2016

ISBN 978-1-904799-68-9

*It would be futile to pretend that all the people mentioned
in this book are fictitious, or, indeed, that the University
of Isleworth itself does not exist, but (if Professor Gray will
forgive me) all the significant actors in this story are entirely
fictitious and are not based on any person living or dead.
Nor is any illegal, immoral or reprehensible act committed
within these pages based on any real events, other than those
which have long since passed into the history books. To those
few real people, including the late King Cnut, who have been
dragged unwillingly into this little melodrama, I tender my
humble apologies, but I am sure they will acknowledge that
their reputations have only been enhanced by their tangential
association with Britain's oldest and most prestigious
university.*

– A de M –

Typeset in the United Kingdom by
TIGER OF THE STRIPE

Printed & bound
in many parts of the world by
LIGHTNING SOURCE
and associated companies

THIS BOOK IS DEDICATED

WITH GRATITUDE

TO ALL FELLOW MEMBERS OF THAT

'SECRET SOCIETY' WHICH

MEETS OCCASIONALLY

IN THE SHADOW OF

ST PAUL'S CATHEDRAL

& (POSSIBLY)

THE TEMPLE OF DIANA

IN THE

CITY OF LONDON

જી

Contents

Prologue

'Look here, Anton,' said Professor Gray as we sped along the Thames at thirty knots in an experimental steam turbine patrol boat.[1] It was a bumpy, spray-drenched ride as we passed the Fuller's Brewery and Chiswick Eyot. The banks here were being undermined by by Chinese mitten crabs, a serious ecological threat, no doubt, but that is by the way.

'Look here, Anton,' said Professor Gray, 'Why don't you write an account of the Madonna business? In prose, I mean. I like your poetry, *of course*, but it's indecent to write about murder in iambic pentameter, let alone trochaic heptameter. Anyway, it would sell better. People like true crime stuff – but *not* in verse.'

I took his point, although I feared he might be attempting a diplomatic approach to my poetry. And so it was that I wrote this brief account of Professor Gray and the Isleworth Madonna in unadorned prose and with the *absolute minimum* number of footnotes.

---

1 The reason for this will have to wait for another occasion. Suffice it to say that the boat had been built nearby, at Slut's Hole, Chiswick, in about 1897 and was the first Thornycroft vessel to incorporate the Parsons steam turbine.

Introduction

OME NAMES, AND even a few topographical details relating to Isleworth and its environs, have been altered to protect the innocent. However, I would like to stress that even some of the more implausible people and institutions referred to in this book, such as John Caius, Anthony Blunt, Polydore Vergil, the Courtauld Institute and the Universities of Oxford and Cambridge, are in fact real.

Readers familiar with the slipshod works of Professor Charlton Mitchelberger will be relieved to find that, under the able guidance of Professor Gerrish Gray, I have corrected a number of his most egregious errors relating to the early history of the University of Isleworth. I have also filled in a few details about the history of Arthur Snakenborg, for which I am very grateful to the archivist of the Worshipful Company of Fruiterers

Needless to say, the main body of this book is based on Professor Gray's eyewitness account of the Machiavellian intrigue surrounding the disappearance of the Isleworth Madonna. Dr Timothy Hutchisson of the Courtauld Institute has done his best to keep me on the straight and narrow in the presentation of the scientific analysis of the painting, but he can in no way be held responsible for any mistakes which have almost certainly crept in.

For matters of culinary history, I am deeply indebted to the publications and personal guidance of Dr Charles Haggerty and Professor Miriam Meersdorf, not to mention the management and staff of the Garden of Earthly Delights in Isleworth, and Eugenie Mablethorpe, Master of St Bridget's. I know that my old friend and colleague, Merlin LeMaistre, will forgive me for disclosing a few of the ingredients in his remarkable beverage.

It will be clear to even the most casual reader that this book would have been impossible without the wonderful resources provided by: the Brotherton Library of the University of Leeds; the Library of Congress; the British Library; the London Library; the Bodleian Library; Cambridge University Library; the Parker Library, Corpus Christi College, Cambridge; the Wren Library, Trinity College, Cambridge; the Wellcome Library; the National Archives at Kew; the Warburg Institute; the Institute of Historical Research, University of London; London University's Senate House Library; the Tate Britain, London; the National Gallery, London; the National Portrait Gallery, London; the Courtauld Institute; the Ashmolean Museum; the Victoria and Albert Museum in South Kensington; and the library of the National Maritime Museum, Greenwich. My heartfelt thanks to all these institutions and to any others I have forgotten to mention. Above all, I must thank the staff of the Peter Guy Memorial Library and Archives[2] of the University of Isleworth for their unfailing help and courtesy. Needless to say, it is always a pleasure to be permitted to delve into the cartularies of Sheen, Syon and Winchester, although how much a knowledge of William of Wykeham's purchase of the church and lands at Isleworth from the monks of St Valéry in Picardy adds to an understanding of the strange case of the Isleworth Madonna must be a moot point.[3]

Finances are always a concern for the modern researcher and I must acknowledge the generous, if sometimes grudging, support of the Snakenborg Foundation whose ample purse is seldom unclasped. I am also grateful to the former Vice-Chancellor, Dr Behr,

---

2 Named in memory of that great and learned man who was for many years the Honorary Secretary of that same society to which I have dedicated this book and, somewhat more fleetingly, Visiting Professor in Isleworth's Department of Typographic Design.

3 Surprisingly, earlier commentators have rarely mentioned the effect of William's annexation of church lands on the University of Isleworth. See, for instance, T. F. Kirby, 'Charters of Harmondsworth, Isleworth, Heston, Twickenham, and Hampton-on-Thames,' *Archaeologia,* **58**, January 1903, p. 341. The uneasy relationship between the University of Isleworth and both Winchester College and New College, Oxford, remains to this day. Had it not been checked, the Bishop of Winchester's soaring ambition might have eclipsed even Isleworth. But that is another story, and one which I expect Professor Gray will tackle some day if he can finish his *Brief History of the Letter K* and other outstanding projects.

who, before his own retirement, kindly granted me a brief sabbatical in which to complete this work, freed from the onerous demands of rhyme and scansion.[4]

ANTON DE MORESCO
Isleworth
8 October 2015

---

4   Sadly, he also made it a condition that I restricted footnotes (for which he seems to think I have a particular fondness) to an *absolute minimum*. I have, of course, complied with this stipulation, although I fear that the book has suffered substantially as a result.

1: Never Trust a Historian

What makes a good writer of history is a guy who is suspicious. Suspicion marks the real difference between the man who wants to write honest history and the one who'd rather write a good story.[5]

NEVER TRUST A historian, Professor Gray thought as he guided his much-loved Brompton folding bicycle through the famous western gateway[6] to the University of Isleworth.[7] Of course, one should never trust politicians, estate agents, journalists, doctors, the police or the judiciary either, and he really wouldn't go anywhere near that bald-headed man at the back of the Clapham omnibus.[8] Historians, though, are despicable creatures, always ready to generalise on the flimsiest evidence, hiding their bigotry and bias below a thin patina of academic objectivity. As a historian himself, he felt it was he was entitled – and obliged – to make such sweeping generalisations in the face of such dishonesty among his co-lleagues. Some of his cfellow historians were so stuck in the past (not necessarily a bad thing for a historian) that they would say – should they could be roused from their slumbers – that one should never trust *an* historian. Almost as though

---

5   Jim Bishop, *New York Times,* 5 Feb. 1955.

6   Followers of the architectural press will already be familiar with this fine Elizabethan structure in Wealden sandstone, with its Solomonic (barley sugar twist) columns and twin bell-shaped turrets. Can England offer a finer gateway through which to enter upon a folding bicycle? This glorious vista (which should, perhaps, be captured for posterity by some up-and-coming art student at the University or by Tracey Emin, Professor of Drawing at the Royal Academy) was, at the moment in question, somewhat marred by the presence of Professor Gray, who whatever the self-image he nurtures in his breast, is over fifty and somewhat tubby. The general effect is not unlike a bear on a unicycle – a sight we have not witnessed in Isleworth for many years.

7   I saw him as he came through the gateway but he didn't see me. We poets are often overlooked.

8   We may surmise that Professor Gray was thinking of the 337 which travels from Richmond to Clapham Junction at intervals which are apparently dictated by the whims of the drivers. The bald-headed man is harder to identify and may merely be a trope. Like Professor Gray, I have made it a guiding principle of my life to avoid bald men on buses, whether or not their destination was, or might be, Clapham.

they meant to drop their aitches. He'd known one who even had the temerity to spell medieval *mediæval,* ignoring the fact that Classical Latin *æ* was usually represented by *e* in the later middle ages.

Never trust an historian (he was beginning to feel that the errant *n* lent a certain bogus authority), he mused as he steered his trusty Brompton through the gateway into part of Britain's oldest university. And there you had it – the perfect example of why one shouldn't trust historians. The man in the street would say, 'Hold on! Isn't Oxford, or Cambridge, or the Polytechnic of Middle Earth, Britain's oldest university?' Alas, you'd be trusting those historians again. The layman didn't appreciate that the founding of a university was a very difficult thing to date. The chances of finding a scrap of parchment bearing the words 'Dear Diary, today I decided to found the University of Hammersmith' are slimmer than a size-zero model. The early universities grew slowly from monkish seminaries into places of real (i.e. secular) learning. Who is to say when they became universities? John Caius's *De Antiquitate Cantabrigiensis Academiæ* contains what purports to be a charter granted to the University of Cambridge by King Arthur. So much for historians. The revered Thomas Hearne, almost as implausibly, published a claim that the Venerable Bede reinvigorated the teaching at Cambridge in AD 682,[9] at which date, mark you, he would have been about ten years old. John Lydgate, for his part, claimed that 'Cambridg was founded long or Chryst was borne.' Perhaps poets should be added to the list of 'bad witnesses', to borrow an expression from the downy under-feathers of the evangelical wing. All these preposterous claims, it seemed to Gray, were devised to undermine Isleworth's status as the oldest British university – the *primus inter pares,* as he was sure his colleague Chummy Beetleson would put it, although Isleworth *had* no equal.

---

9   Thomas Sprott, 'Nicholai Cantalupi Historiola de antiquitate et origine Universitatis Cantabrigiensis', *Thomæ Sprotti Chronica | E codice antiquo MSto. in bibliotheca praenobilis adolescentis Dni. Edvardi Dering, de Surrenden Dering in agro Cantiano, Baronetti, descripsit edidit que Tho. Hearnius, qui & alia quaedam opuscula, è codicibus MSStis. authenticis à seipso itidem descripta, subjecit,* Oxonii: E Theatro Sheldoniano, M.DCC.XIX.

The historian who had really annoyed Gerrish Gray that morning was not Caius, who at least had the decency to die in 1573, but Charlton Mitchelberger of the University of North Virginia at Mechanicsville, a fat and rather unpleasant individual who claimed to be a 'full professor' at that august institution (half of him would be quite enough). Having derided Gray's seminal work, *A Brief History of the Letter K*,[10] and plagiarised a paper Gray had given to the Royal Historical Society way back in 1997, he had really flung the gauntlet down by suggesting that Isleworth's claim to seniority (which is fully documented in Professor Gray's *Cnut and Isleworth*)[11] was unsound. Gray would not deign to rehearse the evidence, even in his own mind, although even the most ill-informed medievalist must be aware, not only of Cnut's charter to the University but also Goscelin of St Bertin's references[12] to Isleworth being a place of scholarship, even before St Mildred left her perpetual footsteps in the Ebbsfleet mud. Mitchelberger's shallow, spiteful and under-researched paper, 'Isleworth Laid Bare', appeared in the June issue of *Educational History* which had flopped through Gray's letter box that morning. That, as it turned out, was the least of his problems.

---

10   Volumes 1–3 and 5–7 were published between 1987 and 2006. Only volume 4, projected to be published in 2018, is still outstanding.
11   Gerrish Gray, *Cnut and Isleworth: England's First University*, Isleworth University Press, 2014.
12   These were clearly inserted to curry favour with Archbishop Lanfranc who had a known partiality for Isleworth. Goscelin was nothing if not an opportunist.

2: Art History is Bunk

History is more or less bunk. It's tradition. We don't want tradition. We want to live in the present, and the only history that is worth a tinker's damn is the history that we make today.[13]

History is bunk, art history is bunkier and art historians are the bunkiest of the bunk.[14]

NEVER TRUST A historian and never, never trust an *art* historian. Gerrish Gray would at least say *that* for Archie Flemyng: he was not an art historian. Many would say that he was not a historian at all, but he *was* head of the Department of History so Gray supposed he must be, although no-one had yet unearthed a paper written by him. In these days of research assessment exercises, he felt obliged admire a man who could hang on to his job like that, only putting pen to paper when a memorandum was required. The last one about the coffee machine would barely have filled two pages of A4 had it been single-spaced, and the wording was so magisterial, so eloquent, that it had brought tears to Gray's eyes.

'Ah, Gerrish,[15] there's something we must discuss,' he called out as Gray tried to sneak past. He was not naturally inclined to sneaking

---

13   Henry Ford, *Chicago Tribune,* 25 May 1916.
14   Ludo Kroy, interview on the BBC World Service, 1 April 1972.
15   Professor Gray has handed me the following note to aid in the composition of this book: 'I should tell the phonologists among you that the G of Gerrish is not [dʒ] as in 'germ', [ʒ] as in 'gentilhomme', [j] as in Göteborg or silent as in 'gnash'. It is hard as in 'gargoyle', 'galligaskin' and 'guileless' And, lest you be tempted to pronounce it 'garish', I should mention that the e is [e] as in 'guestimate'. My family has not had a high opinion of Winston Churchill since the day in 1940 when the then Swedish Minister Plenipotentiary to the Court of St James, Björn Gustav Prytz, asked Churchill how to pronounce my great-uncle's forename (also Gerrish). The great man replied that the initial G was 'hard as in bugger not soft as in gentleman'. When Churchill sacked my grandfather from his post as Director of Plans at the Admiralty, it began to look like a vendetta against the whole family. No doubt Mr Churchill had many fine character traits, but a fondness for the Gray family was not among them.'

but Flemyng brought out the worst in him. Flemyng ushered Gray into the only large office in the department, one enhanced by the partial annexation of a junior lecturer's cubby hole. Departmental heads, it seemed, needed *Lebensraum*, although Gray suspected that Flemyng would rather refer to his expansion of his playground, *à la mode japonaise,* as the Greater Isleworth Co-Prosperity Sphere.

'It's the Madonna,' he said. And, indeed Gray had known it would be, had feared it would be, ever since he had read Mitchelberger's article over breakfast. Even if you were totally unaware of Isleworth's primacy among British universities, you could hardly be unfamiliar with its remarkable art collection, the famous Snakenborg Bequest, and the even more famous Isleworth Madonna[16] contained therein. The University's benefactor, Arthur Snakenborg, had been a greengrocer[17] in Brentford in the days when, it seems, greengrocery was the trade to be in and Brentford was the place in which to practise it. At any rate, Snakenborg had started with nothing but a few radishes and had, by dint of hard work and chicanery in equal measure, amassed a large fortune and a larger art collection. When he died in 1852 at the age of 83, it was found that a love of learning (or, more probably, a dislike of his family) had prompted him to bequeath the entire collection and most of the cash to his beloved local university. This was, as is often the way with gifts from unpleasant old men, a mixed blessing. It was entirely in character that Snakenborg should stipulate a long list of conditions. That he and his advisers managed to construct such a complex and apparently watertight restrictive covenant is a testament to the old man's enduring nastiness.[18] In essence, his will stipulates that the collec-

16 Not. of course, to be confused with the strange Isleworth Mona Lisa which languishes in a Swiss bank vault.
17 Although his immediate family were of the humblest sort (perhaps I should say lowest sort, for though he had much to be humble or self-effacing about, Arthur Snakenborg did not display these characteristics), Gray believes, and I must bow to his superior knowledge, that he was related to Helena Snakenborg, Marchioness of Northampton and maid of honour to Queen Elizabeth I.
18 The successful (and most unfortunate) challenge to the will of Thomas Lancaster (d. 1583), Archbishop of Armagh, on the basis that he was 'crazed and sickly' after over-indulging in alcohol and red herrings, holds out no hope in this case; Snakenborg was tee-

tion will never be split up, sold or loaned, and that it be kept in a purpose-built Snakenborg Gallery within the Isleworth campus. It also stipulates, in a way reminiscent of Matthew Parker's bequest of his library to Corpus Christi, Cambridge, that if a single painting is lost or stolen, or is at any time outside the protective gaze of a duly appointed curator, the whole bequest is void and the paintings and money go elsewhere, in this case to his descendants.

Now, Snakenborg may have been a greengrocer but he knew his onions when it came to paintings and Professor Gray would be sorry to see them go. More seriously from his point of view, his job as Snakenborg Professor of Cultural History was tied to the bequest. On the rare occasions when he was honest with himself, Gray would admit that it was a cushy number – a comfy chair, you might say – and, at the age of over fifty (I couldn't get him to be more precise), he would be hard put to find another post of such prestige requiring so little hard work.

'It's the Madonna,' said Flemyng. 'You've read Mitchelberger's article? It's bad enough that he suggests we're younger than Oxford – and *Cambridge,* for heaven's sake – but if he's right in saying that the Madonna's a fake we're really in the shit,' he spat venomously. 'You in particular.' Gray thought *that* was particularly uncalled for.

'Can't we just ignore it? Mitchelberger's an idiot,' he said, but he knew the answer. Mitchelberger, in a mere aside, a footnote,[19] claimed that the original Madonna had been stolen and replaced by a forgery. The bequest's trustees included two of Snakenborg's descendants, Esther Dalhousie and Marietta Snakenborg. If the bequest were void, much of the estate might come their way.

'I've asked Henry to look into it,' said Flemyng with a nasty smirk on his face. Flemyng probably knew that Gray loathed Henry Hoardice. Henry was an *art* historian. He wore patched tweed jackets and smoked a briar pipe, which items, he had concluded

---

total with no recorded partiality for smoked fish.
19   Surely the world would be a better place without these *obiter dicta,* these unsightly excrescences upon the printed page, at least (I say this in all modesty) in publications less scholarly than my own or Professor Gray's?

from a thorough study of old episodes of *Morse* and other academical detective yarns, to be essential accoutrements of proper academics at first-class universities (or those institutions which pass for first-class outside Isleworth). He liked to drop the odd Latin tag, too, although, as he was an Old Etonian, Gray [20]doubted if he had much more grasp of the language than of his mother tongue.

'Henry's in Florence, doing what art historians do, mostly drinking too much I imagine,' Gray replied on a whim. It was entirely possible that Hoardice was there. Who knew? He might equally be in the London Apprentice or the Coach and Horses. The one place from which he was undoubtedly absent was the Department of Art History (where he had not been seen for many months).

'Well,' grumbled Flemyng, to whom one art historian was much like another, 'Dr Trenwistle, perhaps.'

Hiding his relief (for Trentwistle, being a Rugby player was, by Gray's reasoning, not completely an art historian), he shrugged and was about to leave but Flemyng called him back, 'And don't forget the research assessment exercise. I must have the list of all your publications by Friday.' A curse upon the Higher Education Funding Council for England! The Snakenborg Professor ground his teeth in mock fury and left. But, even as the door closed on Flemyng's sanctum sanctorum, he heard the HoD mutter, 'Perhaps we'd better get that chap Mitchelberger over, too. Can't be too dumb if he gets published in *Educational History*. Keep us on our toes, I dare say. If he can make the time, I'll ask Dr Behr to invite him to the Waysgoose.'[21]

---

20   It must be admitted that Gray himself had attended a school more renowned for its achievements in the the performing arts than in Latin and Greek.

21   Ah, the Waysgoose! We'll come to that in due course.

3: Isleworth, the Garden of Earthly Delights

Isleworth is a village pleasantly situated on the banks of the Thames, opposite to Richmond, and was anciently famous for being the place of residence of Richard, king of the Romans, younger brother of Henry III. In the year 1264, his manor house, water mills, &c. were destroyed by a tumultuous assemblage of Londoners, for which outrage the city was fined one thousand marks.[22]

... the Academie of Manslaughter, the sporting-place of murther, the Apothecary-shop of poyson for all Nations...[23]

GRAY LIKED TO fuss about the research assessment exercise, but it was just a game. He was sure everyone cheated – he certainly did. He felt there was only one person he could rely on in a crisis: Merlin LeMaistre, a man darker (with regard to some few strands of ungrizzled hair, at least) than the porphyritic basalt of his native Jersey, as black indeed as the coal mined by his maternal grandfather (or was it grand*mother*? – there is a certain unisexiness about the Welsh) in the Rhondda Valley. He was built like a bear, but was more hirsute, more muscular, and taller than the average bear. Merlin forebore from saying 'smarter than the average bear' to himself (although he assuredly was) lest he conjure up images of the Blessed Yogi. Merlin knew nothing about art but everything about chemistry.

---

22 B. Lambert, *The History and Survey of London and its Environs*, vol. IV, London: T. Hughers & M. Jones, 1806. To this day, Londoners are greatly mistrusted in Isleworth. Although Lambert meant citizens of the CITY OF LONDON, it is fair to say that this suspicion now extends to those from all parts of Greater London other than Isleworth, encompassing even the natives of Brentford, Twickenham, Kew and Richmond.
23 Thomas Nash[e], *Pierce Penilesse his supplication to the diuell: Barbaria grandis habere nihil,* London: Printed by Abell Ieffes, for Iohn Busbie, 1592. Although Nashe was ostensibly writing about Italy, it is clear that his real target was Isleworth.

Gray also knew where to find him. Since Merlin was now emeritus (though, as already mentioned, his hair was, in parts, still black), he had relinquished all formal responsibilities but was more-or-less tolerated to use the corridors, talk to students and even use the coffee machine (at least, that was how he chose to construe the relevant departmental memo). He had no office, nor even a PIN number for the photocopiers but there was usually a stool in the lab if he needed it. His presence was tolerated if not encouraged by the younger academics and welcomed by those few undergraduates actively engaged in study. However, because he enjoyed the company of students, he preferred to go where they abounded – the pub. And what a pub! How it had escaped the attention of most Isleworth residents, let alone the *Good Beer Guide,* the *Good Pub Guide, A Quiet Pint*[24] and other worthy publications was almost beyond comprehension. 'Almost' because the explanation was actually quite simple; no-one who knew the Garden of Earthly Delights had the slightest desire to advertise its existence, for fear that it would be despoiled by yobs, yahoos, politicians and art historians, if, indeed, these categories of delinquent were divisible. I may even have disguised the pub's name and location somewhat for the same reason.

Perhaps I should tell you a little about Isleworth. For a start, there are two Isleworths:[25] Isleworth and Old Isleworth; and the University isn't really in either but is well hidden from the public gaze, not far from Syon Park, ancestral home of the Percys, dukes of Northumberland. Not that Isleworth is in Northumberland (which is some three hundred miles to the north); it is a western suburb of London. Although the Royal Mail maintains the fiction that Isleworth is in the defunct county of Middlesex, it is, administra-

24 This last-named is even less of a mystery since the pub employed a George Formby impersonator for the purpose of avoiding such a listing.
25 Actually, there are at least three. I understand from my colleague, Professor Simon Crump of Magdalen College, Oxford, that there is a suburb of Orlando, Florida, of that name where 'you will have access to a time-honored lifestyle filled with southern tradition and civility' – heaven help us! I'm pleased to assure you that you'll certainly not get any of that here.

tively speaking, in the London Borough of Hounslow, a sprawling mass of contradictions, bordering the bosky charms of Kew (with its Royal Botanic Gardens) and encompassing the solid Victorian virtues of Bedford Park, the grim, unwelcoming Feltham, with its Young Offenders' Institution, and the helter-skelter noise and chaos of London's Heathrow Airport. This terrible behemoth is what passes for local government in our old and crumbling metropolis. But back to Isleworth and our beloved university: until recently, the earliest known mention of Isleworth was that in the Domesday Book referring to the manor of 'Gistelsworde' but, as Professor Gray details elsewhere, there exists a charter issued by King Cnut in the National Archives at Kew.[26] This fascinating document, written in 1028, refers to the *scōl in þǣre stōwe þe is genemned æt Gistelsworþ.* Unlike many Anglo-Saxon charters, this does not appear to be a monkish forgery. Mitchelberger, who is no medievalist (and some of his colleagues, I know, feel that he even falls some way short of what might reasonably be expected of a sentient being),[27] has stated that *scōl* means simply school but Gray argues that a reference later in the document to the *fēowerwegan* (or *quadrivium*) makes it clear that this was a centre of advanced study. A marginal note about the Isleworth endowment in the holograph of the *Gesta Danorum* adds nothing to our understanding – but what does one expect from Saxo Grammaticus? There is also, of course, Gaimar's amusing and intriguing reference to the University in his *Lestoire des Engles,* something he clearly did not derive from Geoffrey of Monmouth (who is strangely silent on Isleworth) but, presumably, from some pre-Conquest gnomic verses, long lost or mouldering in a forgotten archive (of which there are any number in Isleworth). In 1103, Archbishop Anselm's letter to Queen Matilda thanking her for her

---

26   This charter, a blackened relic which somehow found itself in the Exchequer Records of the Treasury of Receipt, is currently uncatalogued. For an explanation of how this and other unrelated documents may have come into the Exchequer Records via John Bacon, the Receiver of the First Fruits [Queen Anne's Bounty], see Richard Edwards (ed.), *Thesaurus Rerum Ecclesiasticarum,* Harvard University Press, 1997, pp. xxxi– xlii..
27   To be fair, this certainly does not preclude his being a medievalist.

attempt to intercede on his behalf with Henry I, explicitly refers to the *universitas magistrorum et scholarium* at Isleworth in what must surely be a deliberate echo of the early description of the University of Bologna. We know, also, from small fragments and references in the works of others, that both Henry of Huntingdon in his *Historia Anglorum* and Orderic Vitalis wrote extensively about Isleworth, although little seems to have survived. Fortunately, Matthew Parker, with his close links to Isleworth, managed to gather a few of the old documents relating to the difficult relationship between the University and the English clergy and made limited use of them in his *De Antiquitate Britannicæ Ecclesiæ,* as did Henry Wharton in the suppressed third volume of his *Anglia Sacra.*

Today, I need hardly say, the University of Isleworth is a bustling and progressive institution; less well known than Oxford or Cambridge, to be sure, but a name to conjure with nonetheless. A still busier hive of intellectual activity is the Garden of Earthly Delights to which the Snakenborg Professor adjourned in search of Merlin.

4: Small Beer

He has been sworn at Highgate. A saying used to express that a person preferred strong beer to small; an allusion to an ancient custom... in this village, where the landlord of the Horns... used to swear... passengers, upon a pair of horns, stuck on a stick... They should not kiss the maid, when they could kiss the mistress;[28] nor drink small beer when they could get strong.[29]

He was a wight, if ever such wight were... To suckle fools and chronicle small beer.[30]

ALTHOUGH A TASTE for stale beer was not something Professor Gray had ever acquired or aspired to, he found there was something quite magical about the *smell* of stale beer. There was a time, no doubt a more rough-and-tumble and less hygienic time, when most public houses were enveloped in this enticing miasma; a time, also, when the tops and tails of pints were saved and these slops sold to the poorer or less discerning customers (he suspected that Mitchelberger would fall into the latter category if he ever dared show his face around Isleworth). One last outpost, at least, of that bygone era still survived – the Garden of Earthly Delights.[31] The malty-yet-acetic aroma still pervaded the untidy conglomeration of ancient hovels which surrounded the pub, acting as the Sirens' call to hapless academics, postgraduates and mere undergraduates. I was there, sitting in a corner with a

---

28 As far as I can gather, this has long been a precept of Isleworth academics although, with the decline in domestic service, it is now presumed to be defunct.
29 Francis Grose, *Lexicon Balatronicum: A dictionary of Buckish Slang, University Wit, and Pick Pocket Eloquence,* Compiled originally by Captain Grose; and now considerably altered and enlarged, with the modern changes and improvements, by a member of the Whip Club. Assisted by Hell-Fire Dick. And James Gordon, Esqrs. of Cambridge, and William Soames, Esq. of the Hon. Society of Newman's Hotel, London: Printed for C. Chappel, 1811, p. 209.
30 Shakespeare, *Othello*, II, i.
31 Known until at least 1460 as the Garden of Syon.

bottle of Worthington White Shield and a copy of the *Hounslow Chronicle,* trying to compose my Ode for the forthcoming Isleworth University Press waysgoose. Although we were some distance from the river, I felt sure I could hear the gentle lapping of the Thames against its banks, a sensation which deprived me of my usual poetical abilities.[32] I'm not sure Professor Gray saw me but I think that pretty young librarian, Dr Datt, might have glanced briefly in my direction (another distraction). Merlin, as was his custom, never looked up from his pint. We poets tend to go unnoticed in these vulgar and superficial times.

Gray found Merlin (one of the more discerning sort of customers), sitting in an armchair near one of the pub's many overladen bookcases. A pint of life-enhancing, dry-hopped Double Elephant stood on a table by his side, although he had not relaxed his grip on its handle. On the other side sat the young and pretty Dr Arundhati Datt in a simple white blouse and mid-length, slate grey skirt. Her tipple on this occasion was a 125ml glass of Fetzer Fumé Blanc. While not wishing to openly express such overly-protective sentiments, Gerrish Gray was glad to see that she was only drinking a small glass; anything much larger threatened to exceed the daily limit for women recommended by the Her Majesty's Government. In all the time I have known Professor Gray, I have never known him observe these limits with regard to his own comsumption.

Merlin ignored Gray, preferring to stare intently into his diminishing pint, but the girl smiled at him, if a small upward twitch of the lips can be called a smile. For Gray, it would suffice. 'Good afternoon, Arundhati,' he said, trying to hide that hint of excitement which every encounter with the head librarian provoked in him,[33] and she gestured to him to sit down. With the undue haste which only a direct strike from Cupid's bow could provoke in such a ven-

---

32 Especially since I was acutely aware that this particularly floodplain was an important habitat of the German hairy snail.

33 This was not a Pavlovian response to librarians in general (even his bibliophilia has limits), but to Arundhati in particular, although he is more than old enough to know better and, indeed, old enough to be her father.

erable academic, the professor ordered a pint of Double Elephant and sat down beside her. There is a natural eloquence in Double Elephant and he savoured the emphatic note of the Goldings and the unctuousness of the malt for a minute or two before he spoke. 'I'm in trouble,' he said.

'I know,' she replied, and he felt sure there was the hint of a smile, damn it.

'You're buggered,' chipped in Merlin, although his shaggy black-ish head and massive pinkish body still seemed as crumpled and inanimate as the Toad Rock in Tunbridge Wells. 'Overcome your prejudices and consult an art historian,' he added.

'I thought you might be able to help, Merlin. Chemical analysis, and all that.'

'Ah,' he said, 'I see,' and a large mouthful of ale disappeared from his glass without any apparent movement on his part. Merlin Le-Maistre ordered another round while the three of them pondered the situation silently.

'The trouble with scientific tests on works of art,' he opined at length, 'is that they may prove that a work is a fake but they cannot usually prove that a work is genuine. Any fool can make paints to an ancient recipe. I don't know much about these things but I imagine that getting hold of an old stretcher and canvas or an old timber panel does not pose insuperable difficulties to the criminal classes. The best you can hope for from a barrage of scientific tests is that it will not be proved a fake. There is no way on earth I can prove that it is genuine. Your enemies – our enemies, the enemies of Isleworth and the hallowed (though non-existent) County of Middlesex – will hope to prove that it *is* a fake, and they may succeed. We would be wasting our time in duplicating their efforts. In fact, I'm afraid that proving the Madonna genuine may prove impossible – even if it *is* genuine. Your best bet is an art historian. Can't stand the bas-tards myself but you can't afford to be fussy.'

'Honestly,' said Arundhati; 'I can't think what you boys have against art historians. I know a very sweet one at the Courtauld,[34] Tim Hutchisson. We were at Oxford together.' Gray's disdain for art historians (together, perhaps, with a disdain for lesser universities) might, until this point, have been classified as an understandable prejudice, but now he was ready to hate this 'sweet' specimen, Tim (can there be a sillier name?), with a vengeance. There was a more certain near-smile on her lips as she mentioned this monstrous Tim, a slight movement of her body which told him more than he wanted to know. Where, a moment before, there had been a vibrancy, a gentle camaraderie, the hum of voices and expressive clunk of cheap glassware, a sudden stillness settled on the room. The hops seemed more bitter on his tongue. Smoking is not permitted within the walls of English public houses and yet he almost thought he could smell the sulphurous fumes of hell. In fact, it was the smell from a small test tube which Merlin had slipped from his pocket and uncorked.

'An experiment,' was all he said, 'and of doubtful academic respectability,' replacing the tube in his pocket. Gray hoped that this was not intended to be another carbonated beverage (an area in which Merlin had already established a reputation). It really didn't smell at all appetising.

The two ageing academics and the pretty librarian ate a quiet lunch, Arundhati with a salad of smoked duck breast, Merlin a Lymeswold sandwich,[35] Gray a tomato and basil tart with rocket salad. The bread for Merlin's sandwich, a light rye, fragrant with

34 The Courtauld Institute of Art, a constituent of the University of London, was founded in the nineteen-thirties and served for many years as the lair of the gay (or, rather, wretched) Soviet spy, Anthony Blunt. However many agents he may have sent to their deaths during his time at MI6, it is unlikely that Blunt provided his masters at the NKVD and its successor the KGB with much useful material from the Courtauld, unless he gave them suggestions on which paintings to hang in the Lubyanka. However, it is hard to reconcile Blunt's taste for Poussin with Stalin's liking for Vladimirski and the other Socialist Realist painters. I shall hold my tongue now, given Professor Gray's strong dislike of anything which smacks of art history.
35 Where the pub obtained their supplies is a mystery to me, as production of this Cambozola-like cheese officially ceased in the 1990s.

dill seeds, was undoubtedly from the Garden's own kitchens. With such victuals as these, Gray could not long remain in the slough of despond. Another Double Elephant was called for and, in the fullness of time, consumed.

The Snakenborg Professor cast an uncovetous eye over the pretty barmaid whose name, he believed, was Nelly van Nyland. His grandfather, an admiral in the Royal Navy and thus privy to the most bewildering arcana and hermetica of the Senior Service, had warned him more than once that barmaids were wont to eat their young.[36] While he had not taken this literally, even at the tender age of six, he had always attempted to maintain a certain reserve with barmaids. Not that he had any reason to suspect that they would abandon their strict paedophagia for a more generalised cannibalistic diet if, indeed they belonged to the same species as himself. He trusted that the sidelong glances which Nelly sometimes gave him were impelled by urges of an amorous rather than an alimentary nature. It was probably only in this single concern that Gray's thought processes overlapped with those of male redback spiders.

---

36 The following lines of an ancient shanty are quoted in the unpublished memoirs of Gray's grandfather, Vice Admiral V. H. Danckwerts RN, [Isleworth U. Lib. MS Emsworth 172.3]: 'It is the truth, as you know well, | Tho' the song be left unsung: | 'Tis a fact, as sailors tell, | That barmaids eat their young. | Barmaids eat their young, my boys, | Barmaids eat their young. [etc.]' Danckwerts, after a brief and totally irrelevant account of the Battle of the Falklands in 1914, suggested that this text was corrupt and that it was originally *mermaids* who were thought to eat their young. If mermaids were believed to behave in this fashion, it is unsurprising that, in the words of that other song, 'Britons never, never, never shall be marrrièd to a mermaid at the bottom of the deep blue sea.'

5: Isleworth Bulls

There was formerly a very singular species of wild cattle in this country, which is now nearly extinct. Numerous herds of them were kept in several parks in England and Wales; but they have been destroyed by various means: And the only herd now remaining in the kingdom, is in the Duke of Northumberland's estate, near Isleworth, in the county of Middlesex... The Isleworth bulls are remarkable both for their noble bearing and their fiery temperament.[37]

Isleworth Bull. 1. noun C17– An officer of the Isleworth University Constabulary; 2. noun C19 – a ludicrous or self-evidently foolish statement, an untruth.[38]

PROFESSOR GRAY RETURNED to his study to find he had received three emails from Nigerians offering almost limitless wealth and inviting him to provide details of his bank account in order to help them avoid foreign exchange controls. The least generous of these offered him a quick twelve million US dollars. He was tiring of these '419'[39] advance fee scams which could only take in the most gullible and greedy (i.e. Americans) and wondered if he could give the fraudsters Mitchelberger's email address. He decided it was unwise – Mitchelberger was sure to fall for it and might implicate both himself and Isleworth in any subsequent investigation by the FBI or the Financial Crimes Division of the US Secret Service. Pity.

Well, he had to do something about the Isleworth Madonna, so he left his office and wandered through the North Quadrangle to the Snakenborg Gallery. To his mind, it was Alfred Waterhouse's

---

37   [Ralph Beilby], A *General History of Quadrupeds: the figures engraved upon wood by T. Bewick,* Newcastle upon Tyne: Printed by and for S. Hodgson, R. Beilby, & T. Bewick, Newcastle: sold by them, by G. G. J. & J. Robinson, and C. Dilly, London, 1790, pp. 14–15.
38   Aldus Cottle, *A Dictionary of Slang, Cant and Argo,* London: Methuen & Co. Ltd, 1908, p. 139.
39   So called after the relevant section of the Nigerian penal code.

finest work, with the possible exception of the Natural History Museum in South Kensington. Like the Museum, it was embellished with ornate blue and buff terracotta tiles, strange herringbone columns and huge Romanesque arches, but on a rather smaller scale.

It was a true cathedral to art: a nave-like space with a vaulted ceiling (pierced with skylights) held the larger works, while the smaller ones were displayed along the clerestory walls. Even on a dull day, the building was flooded with natural light, augmented, when necessary, with uplighters and spots of unusual subtlety.

The dessicated guard at the entrance nodded Professor Gray in and thumbed a clicker to record the footfall. So much for security. Raphael's Madonna, being relatively small (59.5 cm × 44 cm) was upstairs, on the left, past Leonardo's Virgin on the Rocks (rather disappointing copies of which are to be seen in the Louvre and National Gallery, London). Isleworth's Madonna was reminiscent of the so-called Small Cowper Madonna in the National Gallery of Art, Washington, and was painted slightly later, in 1506 or 1507. It was painted on a thick wooden panel and Gray couldn't help thinking it would be very heavy to move, but he wasn't about to find out – he knew it was alarmed (so how could anyone have stolen the real one and substituted a copy?). He wanted to say 'Do not be alarmed' to it, the line in many a hoary old film (and how he loved hoary old films!), but of course he did not.

The substance of Mitchelberger's claim was that the present painting had a very small structure in the background which bore a marked resemblance to the Eiffel Tower. Gray peered below the layers of yellowing varnish and had to admit that there was a very un-Renaissance tower on the right, so small as to be almost invisible to the naked eye, especially for those of us suffering the early onset of presbyopia. Note to himself: get his eyes tested PDQ.

Mitchelberger was quite wrong in thinking it was the Eiffel Tower, though. Gray recognised it at once as the Crystal Palace television transmitter at Sydenham in southeast London, a far more elegant structure than Gustave Eiffel's crude effort. It was a blow to discover that Mitchelberger was at least partially right. On the other hand, it helped to narrow the timescale. The Eiffel Tower had been around since 1889 but the Crystal Palace transmitter was only erected in 1950; neither, it must be confessed, fitted neatly into the normal Christian iconography and less still into the chronology of Raphael's works.

Of course, one had to ask why someone hoping to pass their copy off as the real thing would include the Crystal Palace transmitter. Perhaps it was the forger's idea of a joke. Great, he just needed to find was someone with a warped sense of humour who had entered the Gallery in the last 60-odd years.

Gray had been studying the painting and its elaborate frame for some time – although what he hoped to discover he did not know – when he noticed someone on a nearby window seat. He was a scruffy but well-muscled chap of average stature in a drab raincoat and, to Gray's untutored eye, he looked very dead – which is not to say there are shades of mortality but simply that there are grada-tions in the *appearance* of morbidity. He was immobile, for a start (always a good starting point when deciding whether someone is dead), and his blotchy, grey complexion would have relegated him to the far field of the Miss Isleworth University Competition, even if he had been of the the appropriate gender and if, indeed, there had ever been such a competition. His tongue lolled thickly, and with a purplish tinge, to the left side of cyanosed, grimacing lips, and a foamy, brown exudate was visible in the margins of his mouth. The sclerae of his eyes were of that shade of pink which Gray as-sociated with the genus *Dianthus*. By his left foot was an empty 330 ml bottle of Nutmeg Cola.[40] To Gray's inexpert mind the cosy

---

40 This nutritious beverage was the invention of Merlin. He had hoped it would make his fortune but, so far, the large drinks companies such as Coca-Cola and Schweppes have proved reluctant to license it. This may be related to his secrecy about the ingredi-ents and some question as to the possible toxicity of the product. Even Professor Gray was not privy to its preparation, although he had observed many interesting deliveries to Merlin's house in Bosworth Terrace: as well as nutmeg, which was shipped directly from Grenada in stout gunny sacks too heavy for the average man to lift, there was dried bitter orange peel (not the common Seville variety but a curious Persian cousin of *Citrus*

expression 'vegetable alkaloid' sprang uninvited, along with countless images of green-covered Penguin crime fiction, musty with
the smell of browning paper made from mechanical wood pulp,
wherein dwelt (beside the ravening dust mites) suspicious charac-
ters suffering fugue states, innocent medicine bottles and sinister
toothpaste tubes, discarded railway tickets – and pawn tickets, too
– and (the Snakenborg Professor particularly relished) drug fiends
whose first whiff of cannabis would send them into uncontrollable
killing sprees. Alas! Where are such whodunnits now? Gray missed
the mad dash (perhaps even hitting 60 miles per hour) in a Lagon-
da and flights from Croydon Aerodrome, perhaps in an Imperial
Airways Handley Page W8 to Paris or a DH.66 Hercules to Cairo.
And, you know, you could be almost certain that anyone (unless
he was a great toff) who spent much time in Paris was a dissolute
character and therefore, in all probability, a murderer. Things were
so much simpler in those days. Gray was thinking of the men, but
the habituées of paris were also (to borrow a below-stairs term) no

---

aurantium) in large wooden crates stencilled with (at least to Gray's uneducated eye)
impenetrable Farsi which probably reads 'In the name of God, stack this side up', for Ira-
nians are much given to invoking the deity in matters of business; dried jasmine flowers
from Egypt and China; the seeds of wild dill from Sweden and the Western Isles; barrels
of molasses from Barbados and India; rosewater – *gulab jal* – extracted from the petals
of *Rosa damascena* in the foothills of the Himalayas; date palm jaggery from West Bengal; dried peaches from California; peppermint extract from Mitcham (yes, there is still
some native *Mentha piperata* to be had in this London suburb) and liquorice root, not
from Pontefract, but Rievaulx, near the abbey ruins; arrowroot from Bengal; spearmint
oil in green glass carboys from a secret location in Somerset; white teas from China, and
Tregothnan green tea from the Duchy of Cornwall; myrtle berries from Suffolk; raspberry leaves from Scotland and finest Persian saffron – none, alas, from Essex; galingale
from Laos and ginger from China's Guangdong province; Totonac vanilla from Mexico's
Mazatlan Valley; *chukri*, or wild rhubarb, from the Koh-e Baba mountains of Afghanistan; qat from Kenya; birch resin from Norway and colophony from Greece; fragrant,
green-dried cardamoms from Papua New Guinea; oil of lavender from Norfolk and
Provence; Benenden Blue rosemary and Fuggle hops in hempen sacks from Tenterden
in Kent; fresh citrons from Florida and bergamots from Italy; cinnamon sticks from Sri
Lanka, asafœtida and black mustard seeds from a Parsi spice wholesaler in Mumbai. Occasionally, crates marked *Ffa'r Gors* would appear on the back of an ancient Bedford truck
from Wales. These are just some of the deliveries Gray had noticed as he cycled to or from
his home in Richmond, past Isleworth's Bosworth Terrace. He also knew for a fact that
Merlin used pomegranate pulp, because there had been an unfortunate incident when a
tanker overturned on the M25. Something was cooking in Bosworth Terrace!

better than they ought. This applied, of course, to natives of the French metropolis as well as Britons dwelling there, but the sheer perversity of any citizen of the pink, imperial bits of the map (of which there were many at the time) choosing to live in a non-pink bit, especially in such a naughty city, marked them out for the most severe reprobation.

When Gray's reverie on antique crime fiction had run its course, he gazed again at the corpse and felt slightly ashamed. He took in the rather solid musculature under his greenish tweed jacket and beige cavalry twill trousers (both rather too warm for the season), the carefully-groomed hair, thin and sandy, the high forehead, blue eyes, slightly freckled complexion and the closely-shaven chin which had, nonetheless, some signs of regrowth. Despite the quint-essentially English garb, his high cheek-bones gave him a rather foreign appearance. The shoes, too, did not befit an English gentle-man; even Gray, who knew more about early Victorian embroi-dered waistcoats, French farthingales, the slashed doublets of the Tudor court and the shoes of bogmen than modern dress, could see that the dead man's shoes were Italian. This was a youngish man (perhaps thirty-five), quite fit, it seemed, before his untimely death. Possibly with a wife and children whose lives would never be the same again. Not only had he died before his time, but it also looked as though he had died in pain. And someone had apparently inflict-ed this upon him intentionally.

Eventually, even Gray's famously perambulating mind felt obliged to return to the matter in hand. This chap looked rather dead (we won't rehearse the shades of morbidity business) and there was a whiff of, if not some exotic poison, then what we readers of crime fiction like to call 'suspicious circumstances'.

This was, at least in Gray's mind (which you will note was now focused entirely on the matter in question), clearly a case for the Kew Constabulary (formerly, and surely more charmingly, the Royal Botanic Gardens Constabulary). It must be allowed that, to the outsider, this very small police force with responsibility for the

Royal Botanic Gardens, Kew, might not seem be the appropriate authority.[41] However, in reality (or so it seemed to him), there was no choice. Any presumed regalian rights in the lands once belonging to Syon Abbey were negated by the granting of the Liberty of the Manor and Desmesne of Isleworth. Moreover, a clause in the Metropolitan Police Act of 1829, which has never been rescinded, specifically excluded the Metropolitan Police from any jurisdiction over the Isleworth campus. Also, in deference to the venerable institution, no attempt was made to incorporate the University into the local government system under the Liberties Act of 1850. Until R. v. Hoadley, it had generally been assumed that, due to the ancient royal hunting privileges enjoyed (but, bizarrely to those ignorant of feudal society, only by permission of the mesne lord) on the University's lands, the Royal Parks Constabulary held sway, but that force was abolished by the Serious Organised Crime and Police Act 2005. Most policing matters within the University were still handled by the Bulls, its own police force – a rather more formidable outfit than Oxford's long-disbanded Bulldogs. However, the Gallery, being built on the site of a former GWR marshalling yard, never fell within their purview, but was the responsibility of the Great Western Railway Police until 1949 and then the British Transport Police until 1961 (in the wake of the Beeching cuts and contingent staff reductions). In that year, the discovery of a decision of the Court of Arches relating to a tithe dispute of 1174[42] threw a spanner in the works. The legally astute will realise that this date is beyond legal memory and therefore should set the questions of ownership and jurisdiction beyond question, although there is some indication (I refer, of course, to Doorman v. Herring) that the ecclesiastical courts, as well as the Court of Chivalry, considered only the period before 1066, not 1189, to be *time immemorial*. However, the unrelated designation of the adjoining chapel as a

41   In fact, as I tried to explain to Professor Gray shortly afterwards, the Kew Constabulary has no investigative powers under the Prosecution of Offences Act 1985.
42   See S. R. Halloran *A Catalogue of Records of the Court of Arches and the Carte Antique et Miscellanee,* Cambridge University Press, 1968, p. 43.

royal peculiar caused the two buildings to be assigned to the Royal Botanic Gardens, for policing matters only. As one wholly (and, indeed, wilfully) ignorant of the law, Gray found the logic of this decision puzzling. But he had been told, and had never had any reason to question the assertion, that the law was an ass. Were the dreaming spires of Isleworth to be subordinated to the palm house and pagoda? Was this great seminary to be engulfed by the Millennium Seed Bank? Nonetheless, he hoped that the Kew Constabulary would, indeed, handle the investigation – the thought of handing it over to the Proctor, Vortimer Williams, and that thuggish gang of ex-cons which are improbably known as the Isleworth Bulls (more formally the University of Isleworth Constabulary) was, to say the least, unappetising. Williams himself, a strong, ugly fellow[43] who had been a sergeant in the Special Air Service Regiment, had always struck Gray as being rather stupid. Merlin, who had served in the rival Special Boat Service during the Falklands War, had an even lower opinion of him. Tellingly, while the SAS's motto is 'Who Dares Wins', the SBS's was originally 'Not By Strength, By Guile'.[44] Gray admired guile but, being rather timid, was deeply suspicious of anything which smacked of derring-do. In any case, guile, unlike daring, is a skill which every tenured academic comes to rely upon.

Reluctantly, he pulled his phone from his jacket pocket and dialed 999 which, as with any such call from within the campus, connected him to the University's emergency switchboard. 'Police,' he said. He would be put through to the Bulls who would, presumably, pass him on to the Kew Constabulary.

As it transpired, Gray was entirely wrong about the police jurisdiction.

---

43 He was described by one American academic who had met both, as a shorter, less cuddly version of Charles Manson.

44 Their current motto, 'By Strength And Guile', appeals less to his intellectual temperament.

[23]

6: Habeas Corpus

'as soon as any slave sets foot upon English territory, he becomes free.'[45]

GRAY WAS, AS I say, entirely wrong about the police jurisdiction. By the time he had returned to his office, the ample form of Harry Haarkon, the Proctor's Beadle was jammed rather uncomfortably into the shabby brown Victorian button-back chair which could swallow most visitors alive. He was helping himself to extra-strong mints from the wooden eagle on Gray's desk and looked slightly sheepish at being discovered red-handed, with his ruddy fist in the raptor's craw.[46]

'I assume that your presence indicates that the University Police are investigating the death, Harry,' he said, without relish.

'Aye, that be zo, Zoor,' he replied. Why this son of Tooting chooses, on occasion, to adopt the dulcet tones of deepest Mummersetshire is one of the many puzzles of life at England's oldest (and, many would argue, finest) university. Gray attributed this, though without great conviction, to BBC costume dramas.[47] While real regional dialects and accents were in sad decline, there had never been a finer flowering of their artificial cousins, Glawster, Cod Oirish (not to be confused with Bog Irish), Mummersetshire, Barsetshire, There's-Lovely Welsh, etc. Even Cockney, which (while almost dead within the sound of Bow Bells) was alive in the former hop towns of Kent, had been artfully synthesised for the television

---

45   Lord Mansfield in Somersett v. Stewart, 1772.
46   I say craw advisedly, for this wooden creature has a second cavity, or stomach, but more of this on another occasion. This black eagle would lend itself well to crime fiction.
47   Gray included in this category the Miss Marple series which, although set for the most part in about 1960, inhabited a strange time-warped world where everyone wore tweeds and looked up to the vicar. The Chief Constable (also in tweeds, of course) was invariably an amiable buffoon who doubled as the local squire – well, how else did he get the job?

viewer by those lovely lovvies in *Eastenders,* not in East London but at the BBC's Elstree Studios in Borehamwood, so that neither they nor we needed to leave our comfortable suburbs to encounter the real thing.[48] 'The Boss wants to see you, sir,' he added in his native tongue, adjusting his tricorn hat.

'Aah,' Gray said.

'They've found the gun,' he said. And that really stumped the great Professor Gray.

'Aah,' he said (for discretion is the better part of valour). 'Now, you'll have to forgive me; I have a lecture to give. Tell Dr Williams I'll see him later,' and so saying he headed for the Snakenborg Lecture Theatre, a dark and soulless monstrosity in the bowels of the otherwise attractive H-Block.[49] His lecture, 'Avoirdupois: Imperial Measures and the Slave Trade,'[50] was laid out as twenty-odd sheets of multicoloured mind maps on Barcham Green handmade paper.[51] He felt that he gave students value for money. Although his lectures were sometimes almost completely without substance, they were delivered with great verve and (if he said so himself, which he did – frequently) panache.

He was the only lecturer at Isleworth who regularly wore an academic gown[52] and he did so only for dramatic effect. Think Bela

---

48   There is nothing new about this, of course. Almost every pre-war British film contains people with regional accents adopting Received Pronunciation (the lingua franca of the ruling class), and almost as many contain people with plums in their mouths making a poor attempt at Cockney, Scots, Geordie, Scouse or Brummy.

49   H for Humanities, you understand. It is not H-shaped like the notorious prison blocks in Northern Ireland (although I wouldn't put a 'dirty protest' past some of our more obnoxious students), but a slim D shape in honeyed Cotswold sandstone, lovingly ashlared and with thin full-height windows in aluminium bronze frames. The whole style is something of a departure for Lord Foster of Thames Bank. Well done sir!

50   *Caribbean Historical Review,* in press.

51   Sadly, this paper mill has now closed. It is hard to imagine how Professor Gray will prepare his lectures when the few remaining reams are exhausted. He assures me that his stock of brass dip-pen nibs and coloured inks should see him through, unless he is afflicted by by a longer life than the others of his clan.

52   Not, I hasten to add, his DPhil or DLitt gowns, both of which are considered rather vulgar at Isleworth, but a more seemly MA robe. 'He did not wear his scarlet coat, for blood and wine are red,' etc. Since it was an Islewoth MA gown, it had actually been earned rather than given away for staying alive a few years after graduating BA, as is

Lugosi. Today he was wearing a yellow bow-tie, an affectation much loved by freshers and old lags alike and bestowing upon him a *faux*-donnishness which he so despised in others, but then he did it so much better than they did.

I shall not bore you with reproducing the lecture itself (Professor Gray has honoured me with its recitation on several occasions, and has made his mind maps available, should they be required). Suffice it to say that it would have been brilliantly delivered and that he no doubt had them rolling in the aisles at his terrible puns and weeping at the truly terrible cruelties and injustices of the slave trade. To assuage some of the national guilt he had engendered, he reminded them of Lord Mansfield's historic decision in Somersett v. Stewart in 1772, the the Slave Trade Act of 1807 leading to the Royal Navy's attempted suppression of the transatlantic slave trade, the Slavery Abolition Act of 1833 and the work of Royal Navy picket ships off Zanzibar in the 1870s.[53] He added that it was the Anglo-Zanzibar War of 1896 (all 45 minutes of it) which eventually brought about the end of the trade in that region. Gray says – and who am I, a mere poet, to question this? – that we have much to be ashamed of and just a very little to be proud of.

He repaired to Senior Common Room, which, since they permitted the ingress of students taking masters' degrees, has become a relatively lively place. As it was some time after lunch and some time before supper, he ordered a Highland Park single malt uncanonically adorned with ice.

There were in far-off days, in Pall Mall and its environs, several gentlemen's clubs, so called, which served – and perhaps still do –

the custom at Oxford, Cambridge and Dublin. Even that is preferable to the practice of some Scottish repositories of ignorance which award the degree of Magister Artium as a first degree. To be fair, few graduates of Scottish universities live long enough to receive MAs in the prescribed Oxbridge fashion, their health ruined by the consumption of local delicacies such as haggis, Irn-Bru, deep-fried Mars Bars and the inappropriately-named water of life.

53   In which Gray's great-grandfather, Richard 'Skipper' Middleton, played a modest role as Navigating Lieutenant on board HMS *Flying Fish* before becoming the Chief Agent for the Conservative Party and, through the sale of knighthoods and peerages, helping them to win the 1895 election.

stodgy food of a type once favoured by the leading public schools. It was, Gray considered, a kind of nostalgic masochism, an 'English Vice' which the French would find far more distasteful than mere flagellation or the peculiar perversions of their own dear *patrie*.

Sadly, the SCR has its own twist on this ancient tradition, for our Catering Manager, Eve Wallander, evokes in her cooking, the refectory not of a *boys'* school but a *girls'*, although the distinction is verbal rather than gustatory. She had attended, I understand, a well-known girls' school in Denbigh, a town whose other major ornament had been the lunatic asylum and it is said that the latter institution furnished a more epicurean table than the former.

The only upside to this culinary disaster is provided by the menus which are enlivened with the schoolgirl argo of decades past. Greengage rolly-polly is Dead Man's Leg, queen of puddings is Bathroom Ceiling, treacle tart is Death on the Tarmac and an ill-advised mixture of stewed prunes and apricots is Mixed Bathing.[54] Professor Gray had never summoned up the courage to discover what Monkey's Bottom was, and neither have I. Sadly, the school which Ms Wallander attended so long ago had no dish to rival the simplicity of Eton Mess.[55] Nor is it only the puddings which are redolent both gastronomically and lexicographically of a former time. Quenelles of trout in a fennel-flavoured blanquette are Brides in the Bath.[56]

---

54   The last surely the product of the fevered imagination of some interwar blue-stocking graduate of St Hilda's or Lady Margaret Hall, prompted by a chance encounter with Parsons' Pleasure.

55   Nor, as far as I am aware, can Isleworth lay claim to the invention of any significant recipe such as that Cantabrigian delight, Trinity College's *Crême Brûlée.* Don't let the French claims for priority bamboozle you – their earliest reference is 1691 and even a culinary backwater like Isleworth managed to serve one to Elizabeth I when she passed through on her way from Hampton Court to Tilbury in 1588. No doubt it helped to take her mind off the Spanish Armada for a short while. At any rate, if she'd eaten a few more of these calorific treats she would not have been able to claim that she had 'the body of a weak and feeble woman'. Trinity's primacy is established beyond a doubt in Charles Haggerty, 'The Origins of Burnt Cream,' *Food History,* 2004, **37** (3), pp. 31–76.

56   Presumably named after the victims of George Joseph Smith (1872–1915), the notorious 'Brides in the Bath' murderer. Gray told me that Smith lived for a while in Pagoda Avenue, Richmond, but I think he was thinking of another murderer, Patrick Mahon.

Having read the menu for amusement, Gray had another Scotch and then set off to find our inestimable Proctor.

7: The Gun is Found

'Forward, the Light Brigade!
'Charge for the guns!' he said:
Into the valley of Death
Rode the six hundred.[57]

YOU'RE OFF THE hook, Gerrish; we've found the gun,' said Vortimer Williams as Gray sat in his visitor's chair. Gray tried not to look blank – that is to say, he tried to look no blanker than usual. Since early childhood he had, so he tells me, cultivated blankness, possibly under the influence of those old-fashioned detective stories in which the (usually titled) investigator lulls the criminal classes into a false sense of security with an assumed air of imbecility. It may or may not work in a criminological context, but I have warned Gerrish more than once that evidence of its efficacy in the shadows of the gleaming spires of Isleworth is entirely absent.

'We've found the gun, so you won't be blacklisted by the Palace,' he chortled. It was an unpleasant sound and the rattle of Williams's dentures over his asthmatic wheeze reminded Gray of a Swedish baron he had met many years ago at a dinner party in Göteborg. The dentures had been ill-fitting and had to be sucked back into place after each ragged exhalation. 'Not that you were expecting to be invited to a garden party, anyway, I suppose,' Williams added in a way which suggested that he would often pop round to Buckingham Palace for pie and a pint with the Duke of Edinburgh whenever Isleworth's hectic social whirl began to pall.

And at last Gray understood. They had found *the* gun, the Chinese cannon captured at Sebastopol[58] in 1854, the so-called Isle-

---

57   Alfred, Lord Tennyson, 'The Charge of the Light Brigade'.
58   What the Russians were doing with these Chinese cannon is still a matter of some

worth Gun. While the other cannon were sent to Woolwich arsenal and what scraps survive reside now at the Defence Storage and Distribution Centre in Donnington, Isleworth's phosphor bronze monstrosity, given to the University in 1859 by Colonel George Key as a memorial to Captain Lewis Edward Nolan who died during the infamous Charge of the Light Brigade, was still intact and (until Rag Week) on display. Cannon don't really set Professor Gray's heart racing, and this wasn't even one of those nice ones emblazoned with the arms of Henry VIII or Philip II of Spain,[59] or a Chinese dragon. But, yes, it was a rather important piece of military hardware and its disappearance could hardly have been more unfortunate. As you are no doubt aware, Britain's highest award for valour, the Victoria Cross is made from the metal of just such cannon, and apparently the government were expecting something of a run on VCs because of Afghanistan or some future war they hadn't yet told the public about. They would soon run out phosphor bronze and the University, in an act far above and beyond the call of duty, had offered its own to Her Majesty. No-one, as far as Gray knew, had mentioned the gun's subsequent disappearance to the men from the Palace.

'I suppose it was medical students,' Gray said, because it always *was* medical students when this sort of thing happened during Rag Week.

'I think so, yes,' Williams said; 'We found it in the Shallows.'[60]

---

dispute. More of that another time. However, it is considerably more interesting than the badly burnt Russian translation of the *Pickwick Papers* from the same source which was previously displayed at Oxford University's Bodleian Library.

59   These are a common as muck, of course, because so many ships of the Spanish Armada foundered off our coasts.

60   The Shallows, more correctly the Shallow Heart of Syon, an inn owned by the Brigittine convent at Syon. It later grew to be St Bridget's, one of the constituent colleges of the University of Isleworth. However, because the University was hemmed in on all sides, it soon merged into an indivisible single campus, so that St Bridget's and the other colleges became nothing but half-remembered names, until the present Vice-Chancellor, Eusebius Homerton 'Teddy' Behr, came up with the trendy (and actually rather good) concept of 'virtual colleges' a few years ago, Gray's own being Wentworth College. Be that as it may, the ancient buildings of what was once St Bridget's (for virtual colleges need no physical presence) have, since the fifteenth century been known as the Shallows, a

'What about the man in the Snakenborg Gallery?' Gray asked.

Vortimer Williams became grave (or *faux*-grave – he seemed to rather relish the situation). 'That is even more serious,' he said; 'I don't know that I should discuss it with you. I know that Merlin is a friend of yours, but I have to say that it looks bad. The man – we haven't identified him yet – was drinking Nutmeg Cola and now he is dead. My men are collecting all the bottles for analysis. It may have been an allergic reaction, a bad batch, or it may be that Nutmeg Cola is intrinsically dangerous – although many people, myself included, have been drinking it for years without any apparent side-effects.'

'Or it could be murder,' Gray added; 'Someone may have deliberately adulterated that particular bottle or administered poison in some other way.'

'Yes, it could be,' he replied with the glimmer of a smile which Gray didn't like. 'Well, I know you are very busy, Gerrish...' He was dismissed.

The Snakenborg Professor really didn't like that smile. Vortimer didn't smile at the thought of bringing happiness into people's lives. He smiled at the thought of their discomfort, misery or destruction. And he seemed pleased to entertain the idea that it was murder. Vortimer disliked and probably envied Merlin, and Gray had thought he would jump at the chance to label Nutmeg Cola as intrinsically dangerous. Instead, he favoured murder. It was puzzling and a little worrying.

Leaving the Proctor, Gray looked in the Garden of Earthly Delights and even the Chemistry Department but it appeared that Merlin had gone home without the therapeutic benefits of a Double Elephant. He retrieved the Brompton from his office, put

name now applied to the surrounding area as well. Because the finest student bar resides in the Shallows, and perhaps also because the Medical School and Isleworth University Hospital are adjacent, it is an area overrun by medical students. Strangely, there are two hearts which beat as one in Isleworth. The other is the college known as the Society of the Bleeding Heart.

a satchel[61] on his back and headed for Bosworth Terrace. The terrace, as you may know, fronts the River Thames, but Gray headed down Grey Goose Lane to arrive at Merlin's back gate. It was a solid wooden affair of some antiquity let into a dense and umbratile yew hedge which rose more than nine feet and hid Merlin's back garden from the public gaze. He was a very private man, when not on display in the public house.

Gray tried the handle but it would not budge. The lock was a simple pin-and-tumbler design and he was just digging out his pick lock from the satchel when the gate opened to reveal Merlin.

'Ah, there you are, Gerrish,' he beamed; 'I'm just enjoying a quiet drink with Harry Haarkon. Would you care to join us?' Of course he would. He suspected that 'a quiet drink' meant pumping the Beadle for information. I was already there, enjoying an unusual cordial, but wasn't included much in the conversation. Poets are not in high demand on such occasions – not in Isleworth, at least.

It was a long garden contained by tall Flemish-bond William and Mary brick walls,[62] with attractive herbaceous borders and, growing up the aforementioned walls, the glaucous-leaved asterions with their yellow, bell-shaped flowers.[63] The plush green lawn bore a sprinkling of pear trees. The central path, of weathered stone, led to a white wrought-iron table and some matching chairs, in one of which was Harry Haarkon slumped, inanimate. On the table stood a tall glass pitcher containing what looked like lemonade, with slices of lemon and sprigs of borage afloat in it. A few violet-coloured flecks hinted at the presence of lavender, rosemary or some other

---

61 None of your modern nylon backpack nonsense. 'Satcheles I will ʒe haue,' as they say in the York Cycle.

62 The terrace itself dates back to that period.

63 Not to mention the lethal black fruit thereof. The asterion is identified with the 'ghostly fruyts and precyous plantes for the helthe of mannes soule' of *The Orcharde of Syon*. The leaves of the plant contain digitalis, the pulp of the berries is harmless, while the seeds contain large quantities of asterazine, a substance which, by other names, is warned against by the ancient Sanskrit, Ethiopic and Korean texts and is sometimes associated with the תַּרְעֵלָה (*tar'elah*) of the Bible.

plant whose flowers are in the 400 nm region of the visible spectrum.

'Harry looks out of it,' Gray remarked. I mumbled my agreement. I was feeling rather out of it myself.

'Some of these herbal infusions can be quite strong,' he admitted, 'and my lemonade "with extra herbs" is far more effective than sodium thiopental or other so-called truth serums. I wanted to find out if I was in trouble over that man who died. Of course, there's no way that there is anything wrong with Nutmeg Cola.'

'Of course.' Gray noticed Merlin's leather-bound notebook open on the table. He could see that his friend had kept copious notes of his conversation with Harry, as always written in a small but spidery hand in his native *jèrriais*.[64] '*Bouôn*,' Gray commented, which was about as far as his grasp of the language extended.

'*Té pliaît-i' d'la gâche?*' Merlin asked in the golden tongue of Maistre Wace.[65]

'Cut it out, Merlin,' Gray replied. 'You know I'm a pea-brain when it comes to languages.'

'And much else besides,' his friend lamented.

'And did Harry allay your fears?'

He shrugged; 'Not really, no. The good thing is that the Proctor drinks a lot of Nutmeg Cola and isn't inclined to believe there's anything wrong with it. I just hope that nothing in Vortimer's behaviour can be attributed to my beverage. The rough side of the pineapple is that his unwillingness to accept accidental poisoning leads him to believe that the man was murdered. Have some cake.' He handed Professor Gray a large Mason's Ironstone plate embellished with the statutory willow pattern design on which stood a bright green object cut into slices; the texture appeared similar to that of what Americans call English Muffins, although they are neither English nor muffins. This, also, was no muffin, and as it turned

---

64 *Lé jèrriais est la langue minnoritaithe officielle dé Jèrri.*

65 This is not strictly true but I am in a poetic frame of mind. Even allowing for a separation of more than 850 years, the language of Wace's *Roman de Brut*, as I'm sure even Professor Gray recognises, is a rather different breed of Anglo-Norman to Merlin's.

out, nor was it English. It was not the sort of cake one would usually eat for tea, savoury rather than sweet.

'As long as they have no psychoactive ingredients,' Gray said, biting into one. It was delicious.

'Oh, they do, of course. Virtually everything one consumes has some effect on the brain, from alcohol, to water, to mashed potato, but you shouldn't expect any noticeable effects from these, except moderate pleasure.'

'I'll risk it,' Gray said, grabbing a second slice.

'I adapted the recipe from a French book.⁶⁶ The French seem to have reciprocated our use of the word *gâteau*,⁶⁷ taking the word *cake* to their bosoms, although I doubt that the Académie Française approves.'

'So what did you learn from our friend, before he was wrapped in Morphius's gentle embrace?'

Merlin looked serious: 'More than I wanted to. Interestingly, the man in question seemed to have rather low bone density. I think I know who he is and I know that I will be the prime suspect in his murder, if that's what it was.'

'Vortimer told me he didn't know who the man was,' Gray muttered through herb, crumb and feta.

'That is probably true,' Merlin replied enigmatically. 'I'm afraid I've already said more than I should. Anyway, we must not let this deflect us from the matter of the Madonna. Your job is on the line!'

'My God! It had completely gone out of my mind. But do they really suspect you of murder? That's terrible. How can you even think about the Madonna?'

'Don't worry about me, Gerrish. I'm innocent, so they can't possibly find any evidence against me.'

---

66   Ilona, *Cakes Sucrés, Salés,* Marabout, 2001. The recipe which Merlin adapted is for *cake à la feta et aux herbes fraîches.*

67   Actually, Merlin used the word *gâche,* the *jèrriais* equivalent of *gâteau.* In fact, for all I know, he spoke to Professor Gray entirely in *jèrriais.* Merlin had plied me as liberally with lemonade as he had the Beadle and I was a good two and a half sheets to the wind.

Gray didn't share his friend's faith in the English justice system, being old enough to remember the Guildford Four and Birmingham Six – and *those* cases were investigated by more conventional constabularies than the Isleworth Bulls. 'I really think we should concentrate on the murder...'

'No,' Merlin interrupted, 'We *must* concentrate on the madonna.'

He was so insistent that Gray gave in. 'Well, I looked at her today. Michelburger is wrong about the Eifel Tower. It's the Crystal Palace transmitter.'

'That's good, Gerrish,' said Merlin, immediately jumping to the same conclusion Gray had; 'It narrows down the time period for substitution of the fake considerably, and also suggests a homegrown malefactor. You know how I hate Continental influences.'

And it was surprisingly true that Merlin, whose mother tongue was what you or I might consider a dialect of French,[68] coming, as he did, from a small island under the protection of the English crown, had a strong dislike of what he called 'Continental practices', which might, in most cases, be interpreted as 'French things'. These could be anything from the *Code Napoléon*, to the ingestion of brandy and/or Rocquefort, or the use of bidets. His greatest disdain was reserved for various models of the Renault Clio, the game of pétanque, and the Golden Delicious apple.[69] The last-named, as he remarked, is never delicious and becomes particularly insipid when it attains a golden (or, rather, jaundiced) hue. Although Gray felt great affection for the French people and their culture, he had always found it difficult to disagree with any particular objects of Merlin's disapprobation. Perhaps it is part of the Gallic charm,

---

68   But Merlin insists that it is a distinct language, unlike Dgèrnésiais, which he tells me is a low patois.

69   Although this vile blot on the escutcheon of *Malus domestica* seems to have originated in Virginia, that fair state named for our own dear Queen Elizabeth I, it has been produced in vast quantities by French farmers, apparently intent on destroying the moral fibre of the British nation and the apple orchards of Kent. It should not be mentioned in the same breath (and probably not in the same footnote) as the Cox's Orange Pippin.

thought Gray, that we see their faults almost as clearly as we see our own.

'You're wandering, Gerrish,' said Merlin, and indeed he had been musing on his friend's Gallophobia. He did find it hard to concentrate with such strange friends about.

Merlin said he would arrange to take paint samples and analyse them. He had already spoken to Arundhati's friend, Tim Hutchisson, who would be advising him.

By the time Gray left with a befuddled Harry, Merlin was beginning to look as though he'd consumed some herbal truth serum himself. Gray wheeled his cycle down the dark lane towards his home in Richmond, dropping Harry off in Twickenham on the way.

He was worried about Merlin. When he put what he had said together, it meant he knew more than he was telling. *He* knew who the dead man was, even if Vortimer didn't. And, with that knowledge, he had concluded that he would be the prime suspect.

Gray was home by ten, home being a small house in Albert Road, Richmond, where all the houses are small, within yards of those twin quadrapedal watering holes, the Red Cow and White Horse. He fed his cat, Pugwash,[70] and went to bed.

---

70   Apparently named after the captain of the Black Pig, but with a nod to both Professor Jack Harris of Pugwash Conference fame and Ann Widdecombe's furry friend.

8: In Which I Tell a Lie

There's no trust,
No faith, no honesty in men; all perjured,
All forsworn, all naught, all dissemblers.[71]

PUGWASH WOKE GRAY, as he always did, at 6 a.m. How the devil did he tell the time? He even adjusted seamlessly to British Summer Time and back to the Greenwich Mean variety, a feat which Gray himself would never have achieved without feline assistance. Perhaps he was woken by Gray's neighbour, Mr Horvath, who seemed to get up early. He was black and white in equal proportions but uneven distribution, one ear and half his face being white, the other black, with a fairly random arrangement elsewhere – Pugwash, that is, not Mr Horvath, who was, as far as Gray could tell, a uniform shade of grey everywhere. It might have been prison pallor but Mr Horvath didn't have enough English to make it worth asking him, and it wouldn't be quite polite, would it?

You may have noticed by now that the Snakenborg Professor lived alone (apart from Pugwash, of course), and you are probably surprised that such a good-looking, young(ish) man with a steady job could have avoided tying the conjugal knot. He had been married once, but his wife, Clare (all the girls he had ever been out with were called Clare or its cognate forms),[72] left him, so he says, for – you've guessed it – an art historian. And good luck to them, he'd thought; it had been a relief to have someone take her off his hands. He didn't pretend it hadn't dented his pride, being jilted for an art

---

71   Shakespeare, *Romeo and Juliet,* III, ii.
72   I tell a lie. It is what we call artistic licence. It's the sort of thing we poets do. Nonetheless, from Professor Gray's rather meandering discussions on the subject, it would seem that most of the not very large number of women in his life had been called Clare, Clara, Klara, Clarry (ugh!), Claire or Marie-Claire. There was, I think, a Caroline or Charlotte or something of the sort, but she seems to have been an aberration.

historian. He'd rather she had fallen under a bus or suddenly discovered a vocation as a nun, but one couldn't have everything.

Today was Saturday and, however much he worried about Merlin, he was going to devote it to the Madonna, as was Merlin, who was taking paint samples under the supervision of the Gallery's Curator, Dr Dave Trentwistle, and Tim Hutchisson. He was ensuring that every aspect of his investigation would be verifiable. Meanwhile Gray would be searching the University Archives for information on who would have had access to the painting and when. With luck, Gray would be able to narrow the date of substitution by reference to old photographs, catalogues and postcards.

Pugwash's breakfast was something which might have passed for gefilte fish (he tried not to look too closely) while his master had uncooked oats with milk and sugar – so much nicer than porridge, he always though. He bade Pugwash farewell, donned his satchel, unfolded by trusty tubular steel steed and headed for Isleworth's dreaming spires, taking the scenic route along the footpath and past Syon Park. A flock of green and red ring-necked parakeets[73] flew, chattering, overhead.

---

73 *Psittacula krameri,* Britain's only naturalised parrot. I like the theory that Jimi Hendrix was responsible for their introduction, but I remain to be convinced. It has also been suggested that they may have escaped in 1951 from the set of *The African Queen* at Isleworth Studios. Sadly (for those of us who like such romantic notions), their presence in Britain was recorded at least a century earlier, according to Sir David Attenborough.

9: Old Ektachromes

I DON'T KNOW HOW much I should tell you about the University of Isleworth Archives. We are rather discrete about our treasures and you will find no mention of them in our near neighbours, the National Archives at Kew. Nor will you find any published edition of our charters of Cnut, or William I's proclamation to the people of Isleworth,[74] because, quite simply, we value our privacy. If we'd had the money to bribe Polydore Vergil into dropping all reference to our institution in his *Anglica Historia,* I'm sure we would have done so. As it is, the relevant portion of the manuscript mysteriously disappeared from the Basel workshop of the printer, Johann Bebel, in late 1533 or early 1534[75] and was never typeset. I believe that one of our alumni was, indeed, in the area at the time.[76] Ironically, this omission may have harmed our chances of recognition as England's oldest university, but at least it preserved our privacy.

The Archives Office may be discreet, but it is not small, occupying the three subterranean levels of the new library block. Gray

---

74 In English, naturally. That unlettered monarch issued official documents only in Latin and English, never French. It is conventional for scholars to define English written after the Conquest as Middle English and that before as Old English although, as you can imagine, it didn't change much overnight. However, the Norman scribes, as Gray has noted in his *Brief History of the Letter K,* were inclined to use *k* where their English counterparts used *c.* It is a strange that francophone scribes popularised this letter's use in English and then expelled it from the orthography of their mother tongue. On the whole, Gray tells me, he is quite happy to give house room to a symbol whose ancestry can be traced, however shakily, through Etruscan k and Phoenician ✦ to Old Semitic, and possibly a stylised ox's head. It started life as the vowel *aleph,* only becoming a consonant in Etruscan.

75 Despite what the *Catholic Encyclopedia* would have you believe, the book was published in 1534, not 1533.

76 Polydore Vergil's petulant letter to to his brother, Girolamo, concerning this event is to be found in the Biblioteca Centrale Umanistica of the University of Urbino. The missing section was never reinstated. The Isleworth section is also missing from the holograph manuscript in the Biblioteca Apostolica Vaticana, possibly excised by the same alumnus, for it looks too clean to have been Bebel's copy text, thumbed by inky-handed printer's devils. The Vatican is almost bereft of Islewothiana, other than a brief monograph by Christopher de Hamel on the library of the Bridgettine nuns.

was just grateful that most of the catalogue had been computerised, although he doubted if all the *rotuli* of the Isleworth pipe rolls crammed into archive boxes would ever be looked at, let alone indexed. After a trawl of the computer, he called up Ektachromes of the Madonna from 1962, a Pitkin Pictorials guide to the gallery from 1959, an in-house brochure from 1981, and a whole collection of postcards from the 1890s to the present.

If you think it is strange that the presence of a television transmitter could go unnoticed for so long in a picture so widely reproduced, I should explain that its depiction is very small and lightly painted. It could also, conceivably, be mistaken for a sixteenth-century wooden tower, of which not a few are to be found in Italian renaissance paintings.

While Gray was waiting for the pictures, he went to the reference room and looked up the annual reports of the Snakenborg Gallery trustees. They were mercifully short and largely of an accounting nature. He noted with interest that there had been a leaking roof in 1971 which had necessitated the removal of paintings to temporary storage.

When he returned to his seat, the pictures had arrived. The early postcards were monochrome photographs with quite good detail and, in as far as it is possible to prove a negative, one could just about make out that, as must surely be the case (since the cards predated the transmitter), the transmitter was absent.

He picked up the two half-plate E-3 Ektachromes and held them up to the light. The 1962 transparency had gone a pinkish tinge, but the absence of the transmitter was clear. It was there in the 1972 diapositive, however. If the dates of photography could be confirmed beyond doubt, they could now narrow the appearance of the picture with transmitter to between 1962 and 1972. The removal of the paintings in 1971 certainly looked promising. This was turning into a satisfying whodunnit,[77] or a whodunwhat, even.

---

77   I must confess that I have been trying to write a crime novel (under a pseudonym, of course) for some years now, inspired by the work of my fellow academic, Sam Wijk, espe-

Pleased with his efforts, he went to see what Merlin and the others were doing in the Snakenborg Gallery. To his delight, Arundhati was there as well, helping the Assistant Curator sift through filing cabinets of old administrative records. Reams of tatty carbon-copies on yellowing part-mechanical flimsies. How long, he wondered, were they condemned to this paper purgatory before being consigned to the underworld of the University Archives, or, worse, the wastepaper bin or shredder?

He told her of his discoveries and she nodded: 'I've just seen the storage invoice. They were kept on a redundant sound stage at Twickenham Studios.[78] Reasonably secure, I'd have thought, especially since they charged the Gallery for three night watchmen.'

Gray became aware of a great deal of banging and clattering from the upper gallery. Merlin was manoeuvring heavy equipment into place before the Madonna. He went to watch.

'Ah, Gerrish. This equipment weighs a ton. I wanted to take the painting to the Chemistry and Physics Departments but Vincent,' he nodded towards a uniformed busybody from the curatorial staff, 'says we're not allowed to move it without the permission of the Trustees. Fortunately, we have the very latest equipment here. The old stuff was far too large and heavy.'

It all looked very large and heavy to Gray. You couldn't see the painting at all as it was so hemmed in with equipment. 'What is that large grey box right over the Madonna?' he asked.

---

cially his wonderful *The Honeyed Words of Dr Onofrio Hornecastle.* Dr Wijk (also a pseudonym) is a professor of history (or something of the sort) at the University of Southern California. Although my own effort is at an early stage, I nearly obtained a whacking great advance thanks to the efforts of my agent, a gay Irish leprechaun called Desmond Elliott. Sadly, the great man (renowned throughout the civilised world for his Queen Mary impersonations and known to his colleagues as the Beloved Founder, or just 'BF') died in 2003. He was recommended to me by John Betjeman's daughter, the delightful Candida Lycett Green. What better recommendation could there be? May you rest in peace, Mr Elliott! Whenever I pass his old place in Bury Street, St James's, or his former office in King Street, I silently salute his memory.

78   Ah, Twickenham Studios! Who could forget Margaret Rutherford in *Dusty Ermine* (1936), George Carr as Dr Fu Yang in *The Chinese Puzzle* (1932) or Edmund Gwenn as Banting in *Condemned to Death* (also 1932)?

'Lead shielding,' he replied; 'Can't have X-rays flying about the place, you know.' And then *sotto voce*, 'This is all flim-flam. Man's an idiot. We have to take the picture to the equipment. I'm just doing a quick substitution.' This did not mean, however, that it would be a speedy process. Merlin obviously thought that he had to spin it out to lend authenticity to the proceedings. It was another three hours before they were out of the Gallery. Merlin locked the Madonna in the Chemistry Department and all four of them went to lunch at the Garden of Earthly Delights.

'Where did you get the fake?' Gray asked.

'There are masses of copies around,' explained Merlin. 'It used to be an exercise they set the Fine Art students every year, back when they taught them drawing and painting, rather than all this conceptual art and other rubbish. You know, one of our students was actually a finalist for the Turner Prize the other year?' His whole face creased in disgust as though he'd just found something rather unpleasant on the sole of his shoe. 'This one's by Phyllida Smeeton. She's now head of conservation at the National Gallery in Washington.'

'Well, I hope no-one notices. We're in enough trouble already.'

'I can't see a problem. The powers-that-be seemed convinced the Madonna is a fake. So all that can be said is that we have exchanged one fake for another. Oh, and this fake has faithfully reproduced the Crystal Palace transmitter. You'd have thought that one or two art students might have questioned the painting's authenticity over the years.'

'I just remember all that fuss when we borrowed the Godwulf Manuscript,' Gray said.[79] 'Anyway, what tests are you going to run on the painting?'

---

79 I need hardly say that the late Mr Robert B. Parker's story about the Godwulf Manuscript is entirely fictitious. This famous Anglo-Saxon manuscript has been in the library at Isleworth since 1575, having been left to us in the will of Archbishop Matthew Parker, along with many other books and manuscripts from Croydon Palace. As a direct descendant of the archbishop, Mr Parker knew this perfectly well and was just intent on mischief, a common failing of our American cousins.

'Well,' interjected Tim, our tame art historian, 'The lot, basically. We're using EDX – energy-dispersive X-ray analysis – and SEM – scanning electron microscopy. We use a lithium-drifted silicon detector – SiLi for short...' He pronounced it 'silly'.

And Gray had to admit that it sounded rather silly and it was his mind which drifted, rather than the lithium (which, as he remembered it, was used to treat depression). He glanced at Arundhati who, to his annoyance, was looking admiringly at Tim.

'...total reflection X-ray fluorescence... berylium window, blah, blah, blah... synchrotron... *Bremsstrahlung*... non-virtual quanta... elemental analysis by X-ray fluorescence... XRF trace analysis... XDF... phase characterisation... blah, blah... mordants used in gilding... thick enough to be X-ray absorbent... attenuated total reflectance Fourier transform infra-red spectrometry... infra-red reflectograms... high performance liquid chromatography... gas chromatography/mass spectrometry... ultra-violet... glazes... gesso... *imprimitura*... underdrawing... gypsum... pigment... bismuth... binding medium... linseed oil... glazes...' If anything glazed over it was Professor Gray's eyes. He was beginning to think that the old-fashioned approach to art history which he had always detested might have something to recommend it after all. It was at least concerned with art appreciation, not reflectograms and these lithium drifted-thingies.

'I don't know half this myself,' said Merlin enthusiastically; 'Just as well we have Tim onboard.'

Gray made my apologies and left, disgusted by the enthusiasm evinced by not only Tim (from whom, an art historian, he expected no better), but also his old friend Merlin. Apparently, the results would take several days. In the meantime, he thought he might track down George Yllingstone who had been Curator in 1971.

10: Sunday Best

One Whitsuntide, to go to fair, I drest
Like a great bumkin in my Sunday's best;
A primrose posey in my hat I stuck
And to the revel went to try my luck.[80]

THE NEXT MORNING, it being a Sunday, Pugwash and the learned Professor Gray stayed in reading the papers (or in Pugwash's case trampling on them in a delinquent fashion). He scratched out a Tory grandee's face from page 1 which didn't upset Gray unduly, no more, indeed, than would the defacement of a Labour or Liberal Democrat politician, a footballer or a pop idol.

After lunch in the White Cross, on the river's edge, from which Gray watched the herons, geese and sundry waterfowl, he went home and started looking for Yllingstones in the local telephone directories. There was only one, a K. Yllingstone in Brentford. There was no reply.

It was a beautiful, sunny day but his mind kept returning to Merlin and the dead man. Why was Merlin being so reticent? Who was this man? Why did Merlin think suspicion would fall on him?

---

80   Robert Southey, 'Botany Bay Eclogues,' 3, in *Poems,* Bristol: printed by N. Biggs, for Joseph Cottle, 1797.

11: Nec Albus, nec Niger, sed Uter

... there is no man but has some colour, but then it can be neither white, nor black, nor any particular colour, because there is no one particular colour wherein all men partake.[81]

When all candles be out all cats be gray.[82]

NEC ALBUS, NEC niger, sed uter. That was Gerrish Gray's family motto,[83] or at least the one he found inscribed on an old book written by an ancestor in Bermuda, and it seemed an appropriate one, for his particular branch of the Gray clan had, on the one hand, lily-white skins which turned to a deathly grey in cold weather and, on the other, very black hair (almost blue-black, actually) which shades to grey and eventually white.[84] Their eyes were generally the colour of Welsh slate, though occasionally the grey-green of Cumbrian slate. They say that blondes have the most fun and sadly, in Gray's experience, the same apparently applied to blonds. He ascribed the fact that women, including Arundhati, usually found him quite resistible – their loss, assuredly – to the cold fate of being a Gray, which is to say, his general greyness or Grayness. On the other hand (and I don't think this ever occurred to him), it might have been that he was getting on a bit and the objects of his affection were generally many years his junior.

As he cycled into Owl Quad[85] on Monday morning, he bumped (quite literally – his Brompton's front brakes need adjustment)

---

81   *The Works of George Berkeley,* Alexander Campbell Fraser ed., Oxford: Clarendon Press, 1901, vol. 1, p. 241.
82   Proverb.
83   There is, of course, an echo of Peter Auriol's *'nec albus nec niger, quod colore medio coloretur'.*
84   On the other hand, the motto might more reasonably be interpreted as 'mixed race and proud of it'.
85   This, of course, is from the Greek αὐλίζομαι, f. ίσομαι, a 1. ηὐλίσθην (αὐλή) pr. to pass the time in a court-yard; to lodge, bivouac; hence, to pass the night in any place, to lodge at night, pass or remain through the night, Mat. 21. 17. Lu 21. 37. The term 'Isleworth

into Millicent Behr, the Vice-Chancellor's wife. Millicent is what might once have been termed a blonde bombshell – think Jean Harlow[86] with a doctorate, a fuller figure and loads of class. She was wearing a vivid crimson dress in some sort of clingy stuff[87] and she also wore, he thought, a rather predatory smile. Nor could he avoid noticing her pedal adornments – those particular products of the cordwainer's art which he understood from a close reading of the great Dr Greer's works were called fuck-me shoes. Things had come to a pretty pass when an unassuming academic (Professor Gray's own description, not mine) – especially one who has no real expectations of amorous escapades – should be accosted by so brazen a hussy.[88] However, he could not pretend that the experience had been entirely unpleasurable. I was passing through Owl Quad at the time and saw this for myself but neither of them noticed me, which was just as well.

'Gerrish,' she exclaimed in a louder and, he would say, more full-bodied manner than he had ever before heard his forename pronounced. 'Gerrish,' she said again, 'Where have you been, you naughty boy?' Sadly, she really did say that and Gray felt he should be wearing short trousers,[89] although he had certainly encountered no-one like Millicent when he was 'but a little tiny boy'.

She was wearing – you must remember that, having collided, they were very close – a subtle perfume[90] which (and surely he

---

Owl,' which you will meet later, has the same etymology.

86 As in the film *Bombshell* (1933). The character played by Franchot Tone says, 'Your hair is like a field of silver daisies. I'd like to run barefoot through your hair!'

87 Don't ask me to be more specific. Other than a passing acquaintance with Flemish weavers in England between the thirteenth and sixteenth centuries, Professor Gray knows little about textiles and nothing about haute couture. Consequently, he was quite unable to give me an accurate description of the garment.

88 That this contraction of the word housewife should have become such an expression of disapprobation is to be regretted.

89 A strange indignity inflicted upon the youth of Gray's generation. He often expressed surprise that some kinky headmaster had not chosen to dress him and his confreres in Lederhosen, but even the perversions of the English preparatory school system have their limits, or so Gray tells me.

90 There is a strange English snobbery relating to the words perfume and scent, the former being considered *infra dignitatem*. However, scent to me is what foxhounds fol-

could detect coriander or something rather like it?) he could feel bouncing around his synapses like a thousand pinballs. He tried to think or at least breathe but this large (well, exquisitely-proportioned) woman seemed to envelop him. It was like sitting too near the front at an iMax cinema; not only did she surround him, he had great difficulty focusing his eyes.

'Gerrish, you really must come over for dinner. With Ted[91] away so much, a girl can get quite bored,' She pouted.[92]

'Er, thank you, Millicent, but Pugwash has panic attacks if I'm late.'

'Well, I could always come to dinner with you,' she said turning away, 'if you were gentleman enough to ask,' and with that she walked provocatively away (in a manner for which Gray believed, though without entire conviction, the Americans employed the verb 'sashayed'). A close escape. It took a braver man than the Snakenborg Professor to contemplate a liaison with such an anthropophagal vision of loveliness.[93] Merlin, he knew, had dared, and that only added to his own reluctance, although he believed she had long since dumped him for an athlete or an astronaut or something equally absurd. Gray's natural disdain for physical exertion made him rather dismissive of those who displayed any ability or inclination for such things.

After a couple of hours of what passed for work in Isleworth's Department of History, Gray tried the Brentford number again. This time a woman answered and he asked for George Yllingstone.

'You're about forty years too late,' she said.

---

low and perfume is correctly sweet-smelling smoke – incense – which is a bit high church for my tastes. Both, therefore, are to be despised equally.

91   Dr Eusebius Homerton Behr, our Vice-Chancellor, much addicted to foreign travel and, I suspect, the company of women other than his wife. If I were married to Millicent, I'm sure that I would also form an affection for foreign climes, although I would continue to prefer Isleworth women above all others.

92   I don't know about you but Professor Gray and I are as one in thinking that pouting, being nothing more than a specialised form of gurning, is far from seductive, especially as it is sometimes associated with petulance.

93   Gray seems to have transferred his concerns about barmaids to the wives of Vice-Chancellors, of whom he no doubt knows quite a few.

'I'm sorry,' he replied; 'Is he dead?'

'He might as well be. Dead to the world, anyway. George, my husband, lost his marbles in 1971. Seemed like a nervous breakdown at the time, but he never recovered. The present doctor says he's got some type of dementia,' and at that she started to sob.

'So he's still alive,' Gray prompted, a daft thing to say.

'Yes, he's at The Meadows in Windmill Lane.'[94]

'I had no idea it still existed,' he said, an equally silly remark.

'I go there every week to see him, for all the good it does, so I can assure you it does,' she said sniffily and cut him off.

---

94 A truly venerable institution. Originally a hospital 'for the better sustenation and comforte of the diseased and impotent persons,' it was refounded in 1673 as The Mad-Howse or the Brentford Bedlam. As Pomfret said, ''Twas both an hospital and a bedlam too.' Even after the County Asylums Act of 1845, it retained the name of The Mad-Howse. Indeed, other than a period during the First World War when it pioneered the treatment of shell shock and was designated Brentford B Hospital, it retained that name until the nineteen-seventies when a surfeit of political correctness promoted the near-anagram, The Meadows. I am at a loss to explain the dropped *h*. Unlike those born within the sound of Bow bells, the denizens of Isleworth retain what, being (almost without exception) schooled in classical Greek, they refer to as 'rough breathing'.

12: The Mad-Howse

To Bedlam with him! Is the man growne mad?[95]

Notwithstanding the recent regulations, there are many private mad-houses in the neighbourhood of the metropolis, which demand a very serious enquiry. The masters of these receptacles of misery on the days that they expect their visitors, get their sane patients out of the way; or if that cannot be done, give them large doses of stupefying liquor, or narcotic draughts, that drown their faculties, and render them incapable of giving a coherent answer. A very strict eye should be kept on these gaolers of the mind; for if they do not find a patient mad, their oppressive tyranny soon makes him so.[96]

GRAY CYCLED UP Syon Lane, that depressing thorough-fare which takes you north from the London Road to the Great West Road and then, under the pseudonym Windmill Lane, towards the M4, under which it passes to emerge on the other side, eventually colliding with the Uxbridge Road. It doesn't sound picturesque and, for the most part, it is not, despite some vigorous hedges and even a field or two. To be fair, it might be the (purely theoretical) prospect of meeting the Great West Road which Gray found depressing, and when he had passed into Wind-mill Lane his spirits rose. He had cycled along this road many times without suspecting that The Meadows was here. Now he looked for it, it was easy enough to spot: a large and rather ugly house of seventeenth-century origins, standing way back from the road, behind dark conifers, it was announced by a discreet sign: 'The Meadows Residential Care Home. Hounslow and Spelthorne Community and Mental Health Service Trust.'[97]

---

95 Shakespeare. *2 Hen. VI,* v. i. 131.
96 William Pargeter, *Observations on Maniacal Disorders,* Reading: Printed for the author, and sold by Smart and Cowslade... J. Murray... London, and J. Fletcher, Oxford, 1792.
97 Spelthorne – who, what, where is that? Actually, I met the Mayor of Spelthorne

He cycled up the long gravel drive. How he despised gravel! It was ruinous for shoe leather and his Brompton didn't like it much either, despite the Kevlar-reinforced tyres. Nor was it much kinder to the undersides of automobiles, he suspected, but before he had time to consider the matter in detail he had arrived at the front entrance where he dismounted. He propped his Brompton against a garden wall of Georgian brick which, had he not been preoccupied by the Isleworth Madonna, he would undoubtedly have recognised as the product of the Heston brickfields.

The drive, front lawn and the exterior of The Meadows were all immaculate, and large swags of *Wisteria sinensis* festooned the front of the building, giving it a festive air. However, exposure to care homes through occasional visits to maiden aunts (like Bertie Wooster, he had been well supplied with aunts, although their numbers were much depleted these days) indicated that the interior would be grimly institutional. Happily, he was wrong; it was bright and fresh, looking more like an upmarket family hotel.[98] Could this really be the same petty-Bedlam which had prompted Sir Cordell Firebrace MP to call for the regulation of private mad houses in 1754? At the reception desk he asked for George Yllingstone and was directed, without any formalities, to the front drawing room. It was an attractive room, looking on to a terrace from which a shallow flight of steps descended to a well-groomed lawn, with the roadside conifers and laurel bushes in the background. There was a uniformed nurse in attendance and he asked her to point out Yllingstone. The old man was sitting comfortably in an overstuffed armchair with a copy of the *Daily Telegraph* open before him.

'He pretends to read, poor dear,' said the nurse, lowering her voice, although he showed no sign of noticing their presence; 'but, as you can see, it's upside down. He always does that. His wife brings him in books, too. I can't think why she bothers.'

once and she seemed rather pleasant.
98   Unlike Professor Gray, I am far from convinced that such a thing exists.

Gray went up to him. He was quite a small man, balding and impish. In fact, his similarity to the late Robertson Hare encouraged the professor to imagine that he would be greeted with the words 'Oh, Bishop!' or, going back a generation, 'Oh calamity!' but Yllingstone just smiled. Gray said hello but no words or movement of the lips interrupted Yllingstone's placid smile. The nurse explained that he was always like that. There was, it seemed, 'nobody at home you know, if you knocked ever so often,' as Squeers said. And yet, here was a man who knew to hold a book or newspaper in front of his face, even if he didn't know it was upside down.

'He talks to me sometimes,' said a cheerful, toothless man seated opposite. 'Doesn't make much sense, mind you; but who does these days? Certainly not that Dave Cameroon, nor Tony Blur, nor that that President Osama. I had a soft spot for that Condaleeza girl. Bit of oomph despite the teeth. She had that Henmania, y'know? All this nonsense comes from reading them tabloids, don't it, George? Rot the brain. Now, George reads the *Telegraph*. At least that's still a broadsheet, not a table-oid. The worst of the lot is the *Guardian*. 'Berliner' format. I didn't fight the Germans so we could have Berliner newspapers and foresprung dirt technique, whatever that is, and brawn razors (now, even I know it should be pronounced Brown like that Werner von Braun who tried to blow us all up), and German cars – German Minis, Rolls-Royces and Bentleys even. And the one's that ain't German're Jap, ain't that right, Georgie? One minute they're forcing you to build railways and the next minute they're trying to sell you cars called cherries. Well, there's a few frog ones, but what're the frogs good at, 'cept running away? Eye-tie ones, too. Always go rusty, which is odd because they were good (in a bad way) with midget submarines and if anything's likely to go rusty it's a submarine. It's the salt water, you see. He loves his hupside-down papers and books, does George. Doesn't realise they're hupside down, of course. I just hope he's too far gone to realise he's that far gone,' (this last bit delivered in an undertone so that Yllingstone would not hear).

Gray thanked the old man for his sage words and decided there was no point in staying, nodding goodbye to the nurse and the vacantly-smiling Yllingstone. It was dispiriting to find him in such a state, although at least he seemed well cared for. Despite the toothless man's apparent lucidity, it was clear that no-one, including he, had managed to engage Yllingstone in conversation for many years.

13: A Don in Slippers

Some with their slippers to and fro doth praunce,
Clapping with their heeles in Church and in queare.[99]

AS HE CYCLED back to the university, Gray mulled over Yllingstone's breakdown and subsequent dementia. Did the one often follow the other? He'd never heard of such a thing, although he'd read somewhere of temporary cognitive impairment caused by depression or stress. It seemed too much of a coincidence that he should have had a breakdown in the same year that the gallery roof sprung a leak and the same year in which he believed the Madonna had been stolen. And there was something else, too, which bothered him about Yllingstone, something which he couldn't quite put his finger on.

He turned my mind to work – the slim but pretentious[100] monograph he was preparing on coffee and the literary imagination. By chance, there was a new coffee shop on his route back, so he stopped to sample its wares. If he had hoped that it would stimulate my ratiocinative powers *à l'Addison* (and who would not hope for that?), he was bitterly disappointed. It was the spawn of one of those grim American chains which seemingly employ coffee buyers with Sjögren's syndrome, or some other disease which destroys the sense of taste, and designers suffering from what Professor Gray called anæsthesia, a lack of æsthetic judgement. He came to this conclusion without malice towards any particular company; all American coffee shops embraced the same characteristics. Gray was particularly puzzled by the fact that they sold decaffeinated coffee. Why

---

99   Alexander Barclay, *The Shyp of Folys,* London: R. Pynson, 1509.
100   Professor Gray assures me that pretentiousness is good. You don't get anywhere in the academic world without being pretentious, he tells me, and this more-or-less accords with my own observations. Personally, I find it very trying and not a little vulgar, but my ambitions extend rather further than the McGonagall Chair.

would anyone enter such a place except to get a caffeine fix? Was it an enchantment with the décor, the plastic laminate table tops, unwiped and uncleared? Was it a devotion to the hideous crockery? Or the coffee itself, tasting as it did of dishwater (although a dash of premium quality detergent would have enhanced both the flavour and aroma, as well as adding body)? Ah, it must be the company, the buzz one gets from being surrounded by mothers with screaming children, the endless inane chatter on mobile phones,[101] the clattering of laptop keyboards, and the sight of the super-obese scoffing with gusto Danish pastries from factories in such exotic locations as Darlington and Dumfries. That must be it. Gray drank a triple espresso quickly and left, his will to live severely compromised.

And it was only then that he remembered: it was 25 June. The Snakenborg Trust convened its board every quarter day or on the following Monday when the quarter day (in this case, midsummer's day) fell on a weekend. Not that Gray was a trustee, more of a dogsbody of the *ex officio* sort. He was what they called an Invisible Curator, meaning that he had a duty of care to the Collection without any executive power. He was merely (as the minutes attested) 'in attendance' at board meetings. So today he'd be grilled about the Madonna and he didn't have any answers.

He manoeuvred his bike through the main gate and nearly collided with Millicent again. He didn't stop to chat but cycled furiously (and strictly against university regulations) across Grimm Court to his rooms[102] in Em Quad, folding the Brompton and car-

---

101   The natives of South Africa, the Antipodes, Brazil, the Iberian peninsular and the north of England seem to be over-represented in these telephonic conversations in public places, but I suspect that they are just louder than the rest of us. No doubt a large team of sociologists is investigating this phenomenon at tax-payers' expense as I write – they certainly have nothing better to do. By the way, Margaret Thatcher may have been a little off-beam (she was, always) in saying that there was no such thing as society (*Women's Own*, 31 Oct. 1987), but she was certainly correct in saying that there was no such thing as social science. Sadly, this does not mean that there are no social scientists.

102   You may well wonder why Professor Gray has rooms in the University as well as a house in Richmond. As Snakenborg Professor, he has the rooms of right. Unfortunately, he cannot live on campus because, under an ancient ordinance, cats and dogs are strictly *verboten*, even Pugwash. The folly of such restrictions is well illustrated by the case of Lord Byron who, finding that Trinity College, Cambridge (*alma mater*, you will remem-

rying it up the three flights of narrow, creaking stairs. He unlocked the heavy, iron-studded oak door and then he could relax. They were, probably, the finest rooms in Isleworth, with mullioned windows looking out over Em Quad, and affording a fine panorama of the surrounding area. Invisible but audible was the Wentworth Chapel where the choir was practising Montgomery's *Oxford Requiem*. Oxford is a university which Isleworth recognises, but does nothing to encourage.

These were comfortable rooms, cool and bright in summer, warm and enveloping in winter, with a fireplace, dingy oak timbers and leather-bound chairs of approximately Chesterfield design. Part of his working library was on the shelves, but what he wanted when he was here was usually at home, and at home he usually needed a book which was here. He had duplicated the absolute essentials – Dard Hunter's *Papermaking*, Aubrey's *Brief Lives*, Chadwick's *The Decipherment of Linear B*, the slim volumes, tightly bound in crushed Morocco *à la* Rivière, of Anton de Moresco's (yes, my own) *Blusher*,[103] *The Man in the Iron Lung*,[104] *Electrical Beauty*[105] and *Pretty Ugly*,[106] the painfully thin volume of Henry Linton's minor poems (now long forgotten by the reading public), Terence Monaighan's compelling *The Secret Life of Weather Girls*, Nancy Campbell's *How to Say 'I Love You' in Greenlandic*, Edward Maunde Thompson's *Introduction to Greek and Latin Palæography*, Elizabeth David's *English Bread and Yeast Cookery*, Michael Clanchy's *From Memory to Written Record*, Marie-Claire Vinycomb's enigmatic *Camberwell*, the pseudo-Bedan *Collectanea*, Wright's En-

---

ber, of the *crème brûlée*, as well as Andrew Marvell, Sir Francis Bacon – of frozen chicken fame – and Sir Isaac Newton), would not allow him to keep a dog in college, kept a bear instead. Having thus adopted one exotic pet, he evidently became habituated to the company of such creatures and travelled around Europe with an increasingly large menagerie. I hate to think how many hapless beasts have been obliged to follow a peripatetic lifestyle, simply because their owners had been deprived of the companionship of a cat or dog while they were studying at Isleworth or some other noble institution.

103 'Delicate and poignant.' – *Scoff Magazine*.
104 'Heartbreaking.' – *London Review of Books*.
105 'Another triumph.' – *TLS*.
106 'Pretty ugly.' – *New York Times*.

glish dialect dictionary, Lewis & Short's Latin dictionary, Liddell & Scott's Greek lexicon, Henry Wharton's *Anglia Sacra* (with one of only two known copies of the suppressed third volume at home), Josephus's Ἰουδαϊκὴ Ἀρχαιολογία and the complete works of Shakespeare, Lu Hsun and Rabindranath Tagore.

There were some types of blotterature[107] which would be forever banished from Gray's creaking shelves, including the works of the pretentious Umberto Eco,[108] Elizabeth Eisenstein's mind-numbingly boring *The Printing Revolution in Early Modern Europe*,[109] and anything by modern French philosophers. He did, however, find space for Sokal and Bricmont's *Impostures Intellectuelles*.

Here, also, he kept his signed copies of Bernal's *Black Athena*, Julia Lacey Brooke's *The Stoic, the Weal and the Malcontent*, Harry Bhadeshia's *Bainite in Steels*, Michael Harvey's *Adventures with Letters*, and the same author's photographic essays on *Bicycles* and *Hydrants* (the last is a work which will achieve new significance if Professor Gray follows his monograph on the letter K with one on the letter H), Simon Crump's *John Company and the Despoilment of India* and Jo Jacomb's *Representations of Theories of Time in the Work of Diana Wynne Jones*. A spare and imperfect copy of *Anglia Sacra* volume I acted as a door-stop to the kitchen (I refuse to give it the official Isleworth University designation of 'kitchenette') and the 1768 edition of the *Encyclopaedia Britannica*, along with volumes I, II and IV of the 1694 edition of the *Dictionnaire de l'Académie Française*, stood in for the broken right fore-leg of

---

107   Had John Colet (1467–1519), Dean of St Paul's and founder of St Paul's School, left us no other monument than the coining of this word, he would still have done enough to earn his place in history, and our hearts. It is a word I use nearly every day and I cannot understand how it has failed to find its way into the *Oxford English Dictionary*.

108   Personally, I rather enjoyed *The Name of the Rose,* and feel that anyone whose father was an accountant and whose major literary influence is Jorge Luis Borges deserves our sympathy – he has mine, if not Professor Gray's, for he is incensed that Eco's book has outsold the available volumes of *A Brief History of the Letter K*.

109   If you really want a sleeping draft, Professor Gray tells me that you could do worse than read Johan Huizinga's *Herfsttij der Middeleeuwen*, Haarlem: H. D. Tjeenk Willink, 1919. Anglophone insomniacs will be pleased to know that it was translated into English as *The Waning of the Middle Ages* and is still available.

Gray's desk. There was nothing so soothing as being surrounded by familiar books. And he needed soothing, with the prospect of a meeting of the Snakenborg Trustees in the afternoon. It was a little like being summoned to attend a meeting of the Star Chamber at the best of times and, with the Madonna missing, this was not the best of times. He put on a pair of his Persian slippers[110] (which, unlike Sherlock Holmes, he did not dedicate to the storage of pipe tobacco) and picked up Gratien's *Pantofla Decretorum* to take his mind off worldly matters, which it assuredly did.

---

110   I do not know about Persian slippers in general, but I have noticed that Professor Gray's several pairs of slippers are of identical design for left and right feet. Hence, Bertrand Russell's observation that, 'The Axiom of Choice is necessary to select a set from an infinite number of socks, but not an infinite number of shoes,' would put Gray's slippers firmly in the sock camp, however much they might seem to be shoe-like. It is possible that Russell, coming from the rather sheltered upper echelons of society, was unfamiliar with slippers which are neither right- nor left-footed. It seems equally likely that he was unaware that some hiking socks are different for left and right feet and should, therefore, be treated, in relation to the Axiom, as shoes. I need hardly say, in any case, that Professor Gray's collection of slippers is *finite*. It is also extremely unlikely that he has ever owned a pair of hiking socks.

14: A Kiss Curl and a Cow Lick

... and afore the denudate dome he sported
Not a kiss-curl but a cow-lick...[111]

PROFESSOR GRAY WALKED without much enthusiasm across the glorious Em Quad with its magnolia grandiflora to the grim Snakenborg Building.[112] The exterior was quite hideous enough to give even a typically philistine RIBA member nightmares (and there are few more philistine than the average British architect), but the inside was much worse. The boardroom was completely windowless, lit by fluorescent tubes which, apart from causing epileptic fits among a few unfortunates, look dreadful and cast an unkind light on those with less than flawless complexions. The carpets were thick and synthetic, generating static and deadening all sound (other than the hiss of defective fluorescent tubes). The Eames La Fonda chairs, as Gray remarked to me at the time, seamlessly married ugliness with unrivalled discomfort.

By way of compensation there was an aroma of freshly-brewed coffee – Monsooned Malabar, if his nose did not deceive him. He helped himself and confirmed the identification. The others present were Big Dave Trentwistle, the Director of the Snakenborg Gallery, a solicitor he disliked called Julius Madderbourne, Dr Lynda Brockbank, the frighteningly intellectual Professor of Industrial Design, Alison Guy from the Finningham Gallery, Mr John Parfitt of the University Press and the two surviving members of the Snakenborg greengrocery dynasty, Esther Dalhousie and Marietta Snakenborg. And I was there – it's a Buggin's turn sort of thing which even po-

---

111   Henry Lavington, *Flax,* London: Longman, 1863, p. 74.

112   Not by any means Le Corbusier's finest effort. Shuttered concrete doesn't lend itself to the damp Isleworth microclimate. Frankly, if architects want 'wood effect', they should use wood not concrete. I prefer the vision, though not the build quality of Nikolai Sutyagin's dacha in sunny Архангельск.

ets cannot hope to escape, not that my opinions are often (if ever) sought. Esther was a dreary specimen with the remnants of what might in girlitude have been mere plainness, now transformed by time and temperament, abetted by almost-luminescent orange hair dye and face powder of an ochre hue, into unalloyed ugliness. Deep furrows on her brow and a downturned mouth testified to habitual sullenness (a trait which Gray could confirm from his own observations), and garish lipstick failed to lend a false imprint[113] of loveliness to her thin lips. If there was such a thing as wilful ugliness (and Gray felt sure there was), this was it. She sat in a corner with a look which could (and surely would) curdle milk and Gray was thankful that he took his coffee black.

Her cousin Marietta was a different proposition. She is blonde and pretty in a silly sort of way – Is there any other way to be both blonde and pretty? Perhaps, but not within the confines of this book. Her golden hair, which was either natural or expertly tinted,[114] had (to his taste, and speaking or at least thinking, as he was, parenthetically) far too many curls and ringlets. It was an impractical style (as some impatient reviewers have said also of my poetry) which seemed to show, like the long fingernails of some eastern cultures, a disdain for even the lightest labour or, as Lady Bracknell would say, a contempt for the ordinary decencies of family life. Nonetheless, she was pretty and her smile could be warm, if perhaps artificial.

Today she was wearing the famous Snakenborg Charms, the ostentatious diamond-and-emerald necklace and matching earrings which were such dazzling examples of Victorian conspicuous consumption.[115] She had contrived to sit in a pool of light, while those

113   I use the term, at least in part, in the bibliographical sense. See Birgitte Holck, *False Imprints in Eighteenth-Century French Political Tracts*, København: Elfinbrot, 1977. How I mourn the passing of the ancient publishing house of Elfinbrot! I hasten to add that the great Dr Holck shares none of Ms Dalhousie's physical or character traits.

114   It is my understanding that the fairer sex, who are often fair through artifice rather than genetics, prefer the word 'tinted' to 'dyed' but a rose by any other name...

115   The name, I believe, was originally applied not to the baubles but the ample charms of Mrs Arthur Snakenborg. The jewels, however, seem to predate the family's adven-

around her were in obscurity and when Gray sat next to her and, in every sense, in her shadow, she smiled sweetly at him. As he swept back an unruly forelock,[116] she remarked in a playful way, 'There is a fine line, Professor Gray, between a kiss curl and a cow lick.' What an earth was that supposed to mean? Was she being coquettish or insulting? Did he care?

'You drink your coffee black, Professor, Gray?' she continued.

'I do, Miss Snakenborg,' he replied. It was a very old-fashioned exchanged and he felt he should have addressed her as ma'am. 'Milk in coffee is a crime against nature, as heinous as putting milk in scrambled eggs,[117] or port on stilton.'[118]

'But don't you love traditional French coffee with hot milk?'

'Well, yes, if you can get it, but it has to be *French* coffee and *Norman* milk, nothing else will do; even the Charentais stuff will not do. The best coffee I ever tasted was that we had for breakfast at the University of Caen when I was an undergraduate. It was ladled, already mixed with milk, from a steaming stainless steel vat of remarkable ordinariness. That and some bread with Isigny butter was all we had, or ever wanted, for breakfast. There was nothing else to recommend the university gastronomically or intellectually, as I recall.'

'So – at least in the matter of coffee – you are not a man of unbending principles.'

'I've no idea,' Gray said rather petulantly, hoping to end this perplexing discussion.

---

tures into greengrocery, a matter I shall discuss further in my forthcoming volume, *The Snakenborg Charms*. I should add that Marietta's décolletage on this occasion did nothing to disgrace the family tradition.

116 As I may have mentioned, the males of Professor Gray's family are blessed (in youth, at least) with a superabundance of inky black hair. It is somewhat inclined to flop over the forehead, giving the males of the species a certain appearance of foppishness, even after their hair turns grey.

117 One unfortunate cook at Buckingham Palace lost his job for this appalling culinary *faux pas*.

118 It is hard to disagree with Professor Gray on this last point; port and stilton is a marriage made in hell and an invention of unmitigated vulgarity.

Madderbourne called the meeting to order. It started with the presentation of accounts. As always, the Trust had more money than it knew what to do with. After the Wellcome Trust, it was possibly the largest charitable institution in the UK. Unlike Wellcome, it has no clear *raison d'être,* other than to perpetuate the art gallery and maintain Pugwash and and Professor Gray in the manner to which they had become accustomed. Gray didn't think that either he or his feline sidekick were likely to make much of a dent in four billion pounds, and the gallery spent exactly nothing on acquisition.[119] Nor had they, it was beginning to seem, spent much on security or roof maintenance. Madderbourne droned on and Gray's mind wandered, as (it must be confessed) it so often did – money, was that the motive for stealing the Madonna? How would anyone ever sell such a famous painting? While he was on the subject of money, it suddenly occurred to him for the first time that Merlin LeMaistre had an awful lot of it. He was famous for his fast cars, fast women and exotic holidays. Whilst the average academic might be able to afford a hot hatch, a spouse who buys rather more chocolate than he/she really needs, and a short break in Tuscany, Merlin's taste ran more to Aston Martins, women who liked to drip with diamonds and long holidays in the furthest corners of the earth. He knew that Merlin had recently pre-ordered the Morgan LIFECar,[120] his fling with Millicent could only be considered a liability in every sense, and he had recently returned from a short walk in the Hindu Kush with a rather charming lady from Baluchistan who was said to be an expert on oriental carpets. I shall not bore you with a full account of the meeting of the Trustees, which I found both perplexing and rather dull. I had hoped to augment my account by reference to the minutes but these are not made public, even to those in attendance. Unfortunately, Professor Gray also seems to have taken little notice of the proceedings. At least, he was unable to provide me with a

---

119 Like the Wallace Collection, the contents of the gallery are 'closed': nothing can be added to it or removed from it, a fact which made the switching of the Madonna all the more embarrassing.

120 A rather odd-looking sports car powered by hydrogen fuel cells.

fuller account than I give here and which I pieced together from my own recollections.

The matter of the Madonna was touched upon, but quickly dropped when Gray assured those present that it bore no depiction of the Eiffel Tower. He did not feel it was incumbent upon him to raise the matter of the Crystal Palace transmitter. The meeting ended in its usual desultory way.

He strode out, gasping for fresh air and yearning for natural light. Just as he had inhaled his first lungful of clean Isleworth hydrogen, oxygen, nitrogen, carbon dioxide, carbon monoxide, hydrogen sulphide and sundry airborne particulates, just as the first glimmer of tepid sun struck his forehead, he felt the left arm of his jacket snag and he looked down to see a small, featureless hand detaining the delicate silk–linen fabric above the elbow. He was shocked and vaguely repelled on tracing this waxy, doll-like limb to its origin and discovering that it belonged to Marietta Snakenborg. He had never before noticed that this woman had such characterless hands and it disturbed him, although hardly more so than the unsmiling presence of her hideous cousin Esther. 'We need to talk, Professor,' said Marietta, 'About the painting. It will change everything, you know, if it has disappeared – for all three of us.'

'Oh, don't worry about that,' said Gray, perhaps not exercising as much caution as he should have, considering that he had abetted the painting's illicit removal, 'The Madonna is safe, the Collection is safe. There is no question of that. There has just been a little misunderstanding. It may take a week or two to sort out, that's all.'

'But,' said Marietta, 'Even if it reappears, the temporary absence would surely invalidate the bequest to the University.' Not unnaturally, since she stood to inherit more than two billion pounds Sterling if the terms of the bequest were broken, she seemed to find the idea appealing and it brought a radiance to her face which almost managed to erase the awful memory of her doll-like hand. Even Esther almost smiled but it did nothing to improve her appearance.

'You might think so but I do not,' said Gray, 'You can always ask a solicitor.' He marched away, giving them a hearty wave and the brightest smile he could simulate. I followed him at a safe distance, a sort of Isleworthian Boswell, perhaps.

Exhausted by the meeting and its aftermath, Gray strolled very slowly several times around Em Quad. It really was *very* slowly and in the end I crept away and left him to his own devices. Had he been an Oxford undergraduate in the days of Doctor Fell, he would have been called a scobolotcher,[121] something a little like what we at Isleworth call an owl,[122] but the ambulation did nothing to aid the ratiocinative processes and he returned to his rooms weighed down by concerns about the Madonna and Merlin.

---

121   An undergraduate, hands in pockets, walking round a quadrangle, deep in thought and/or counting trees. I need hardly remind the reader that tree-counting, like doodling, is a recognised concentration technique which relies on left/right brain co-ordination.

122   See my previous footnote about the origin of the word 'owl'. Unlike the Oxonian word, an Isleworth owl need not be an undergraduate. Many a distinguished professor and several gardeners have been owls. Although not an Isleworthian, John Tradescant (several items from whose Ark found their way into our collections) is regarded by us as an honorary owl. The great painter J. M. W. Turner is known to have spent many evenings in 1804 and 1805, when living at Syon Ferry House, wandering around our various quads, and is therefore listed among the eminent owls whose names are engraved onto the oak panelling of the Old South Library in Em Quad. In 1706 Chief Rabbi Aaron Hart (Uri ben Rav Hirz Hamburger) is said to have questioned his conscience about the Ascher Cohen divorce case while wandering around Bleeding Heart Quad, though neither the wooden panels nor Hart's *Urim v'tumin* (1707) bears testament to this assertion. Professor Gray, while not yet celebrated thus in chiseled letters (for which he may be thankful – only the dead are so commemorated), has the reputation of an owl. His advanced use of columns in this regard is mentioned later in the book.

15: Treacle in Gilead

Is there – is there balm in Gilead? – tell me – tell me, I implore![123]

Is there no tryacle in Gilead?[124]

GERRISH GRAY AND Merlin LeMaistre were sitting in Merlin's garden in the shade of an ancient Mongolian lime.[125] They were drinking the 2004 vintage of the cider Merlin made at his farm near Stroud, where he also kept Gloucester Old Spots. I happened to be walking past and glimpsed them through a gap in the yew hedge.

'Pigs and apples always go together,' Merlin told Gray, 'My porkers love the taste of cider apples (we use mostly Dymock Red, Ansell and Bushy French), although Flossy (she's my favourite sow – I know I shouldn't have favourites) prefers Gascoyne's Scarlets and Archie likes Worcester Pearmains, God bless him. I tried making cider from Worcester Pearmains once. Rather disappointing. You need more acidity for a good cider.'

'Did you inherit the farm?' Gray asked, feeling that, as an old friend, he should already know.

'Lord no! The only thing I ever inherited was an inquisitive mind. My father, you know, came from very humble stock. But he was a clever man with a fascination for obscure facts – a bit like you, Gerrish, although his head was screwed on a lot more tightly. No, I

---

123 Edgar Allan Poe, *The Raven*.
124 Jeremiah, 8. 22 (*Beck's Bible*)
125 The flowers of which Merlin uses to make a herbal tea, possessing, he claims, antispasmodic properties – though neither he nor Gerrish Gray is given to spasms. Perhaps he even includes them in his nutmeg cola. Unfortunately, it smells (and I can state this with some authority) like pre-Glasnost aftershave from one of the Baltic states. No doubt this sickly odour helps to attract pollinating insects but it has no proven benefits with regard to the mating rituals of humans.

bought the farm in 2001. Made some money at the beginning of the dot-com bubble You know what the Yen carry-trade is?

'A Japanese take-away?' Asked Gray with no great expectation of being correct.

Merlin scowled because he thought his old friend was being supercilious (I could see him scowl, even through the hole in the hedge). Gray wasn't be supercilious, although it came naturally enough. He considered himself a bear of little brain with no understanding of financial shenanigans and with this, I think, most of his colleagues would concur.

'It's odd,' Merlin continued in his rambling way, 'how the Japanese, so successful in some ways, have made such a hash of their economy, although not as much as we have. The point is, Gerrish, that the Japanese Central Bank Discount Rate in February 1999 was half a percent and banks were actually charging customers to keep their money in savings accounts. Here the Bank Rate was six percent. In theory, you could borrow in Japan, put the money in a British savings account and make several percent interest on money you didn't own, as long as the Yen didn't appreciate too much against Sterling. But I didn't do that.'

'No?' Gray said by way of encouragement.

'No, I bought shares in a Californian dot-com company.'

Gray was a little surprised by this as Merlin had openly scoffed at people who ploughed money into dot-com companies. But then, as Merlin had told him many times, the secret of investing was to know not only what to buy but when, not to mention when to sell. At least it explained where his money came from – it certainly wasn't from sales of nutmeg cola.

'I wish my mortgage were in Yen,' Gray said.[126]

126   As Merlin subsequently pointed out to to his friend, the consequences of a Yen mortgage would have been catastrophic to him in the aftermath of the credit crunch and Sterling's precipitous fall against the Yen. If he had taken out a £100,000 mortgage in July 2008, that would have equated to ¥21.5m. By the end of the year, his mortgage would have grown in Sterling terms to about £163,000 and, even allowing for a small reduction in interest rates, his monthly repayments would probably increased by about 60%.

'My farm's mortgage was, but I paid it off when I thought the Yen might start to appreciate,' Merlin replied. Gray had been about to ask him how he'd done it when he dragged a large and heavy parcel from behind a bay tree.

'Happy Birthday, Gerrish. I hope you like it.'

Gray had completely forgotten that it was his birthday. 'It' turned out to be a case of Cos d'Estournel 2000, a very good year and an extremely generous gift. Gray was particularly fond of St Estèphe.

'Thank you, Merlin. That's extremely generous of you,' he said

'Not at all, Gerrish. To be honest, I'm making way for a dozen cases of Chateau Lafite 2005[127] which are winging their way from Berry Brothers and Rudd as we speak.' Gray's mind boggled. That sounded like about £80,000-worth of wine which he wouldn't even touch until 2020. The total contents of Merlin's cellar were probably worth more than his house, or his farm.

'I'd have given you a flitch of bacon from my Old Spots,' he continued, 'but I always felt that there was something faintly rather Rabbinical about you.'[128]

'Heard any more about the dead man?'

'Indeed, no,' Merlin replied, shaking his shaggy head like a wet dog.

---

127 Merlin, you will perceive, is a Pauillac man. It is an expensive taste and one which Professor Gray has vowed to avoid acquiring, although he has been known to sip a glass of Ch. Lafite at gunpoint, literally, but that's another story. Gray once had some of Merlin's 1888 vintage, bottled by Prytz & Co. Well past its best, he thought.

128 It could not have been be the beard or yarmulka or tallit, all three of which were absent, nor, as far as I am aware, Gray's ancestry – but who knows? It cannot be ascribed to his interest in Judaism, for he has no interest in any religion, something of a drawback for a cultural historian. Perhaps Merlin was influenced by Gray's occasional habit of writing from right to left, but he more commonly adopted the βουστροφηδόν approach (which is to say, alternating directions like oxen ploughing fields) of several ancient civilizations, appreciating as he did the economy of motion – for one is saved the drudgery of returning to the left (or right) at the end of each line. Gray tells me that he cannot read a word of Hebrew, and that he can, as Denkmann put it, swear but little in Yiddish or Ladino – something he feels it is incumbent upon him to remedy in the near future, although the pleasure-grounds of Isleworth may not be the most suitable environment in which to pursue such aspirations.

[66]

By this time, the cider was meandering its way (in the pre-scribed fashion) across the blood–brain barrier so that the sight of two muscle-bound Isleworth Bulls in full fig (which is to say navy blue serge of a particularly robust weave) marching up the garden path seemed more amusing than alarming to Professor Gray, even though their shiny, Goodyear-welted, regulation-issue size twelves looked most inappropriate on the daisy-strewn lawn.

One of the officers, 'Stomper' Harris, who looked like the Incredible Hulk on steroids, but more inclined to a vermilion than a verdant hue, spoke with the timbre of a fog horn encased in oak and with the ponderous delivery taught (one can only assume) at Hendon Police College: 'Merlin LeMaistre, I am arresting you for the murder of, er an individual yet to be identified – you know who I'm referring to. You do not have to say anything, but it may harm your defence if you do not mention when questioned something which you later rely on in court. Anything you do say may be taken down and given in evidence.' He wiped his brow, sweating from the profound mental effort of summoning up the cautionary words.

'I'll come quietly; you've got me bang to rights, Guv,' said Merlin with customary levity. 'May I gather up a toothbrush and some pyjamas?'

'I'd better come with you,' said Harris. 'Don't want you absconding.'

Gray was left with a quiet and gentle soul called Bill Haddow and ascertained without delay that Merlin was being arrested on the basis that: (1) the victim had been poisoned by some (as yet unidentified) botanical substance; (2) a typed note found in the victim's pocket bore the inscription, 'Gallery 1 p.m. – M'; and most damningly (3) a playing card. It was the Queen of Hearts but the Qs and hearts in top left and bottom right[129] corners were not red but black.

---

129 I confess to being surprised that the cards were double-headed, unlike most De La Rue cards of the period. Perhaps Professor Gray will enlighten us on this matter in one of his amusing contribution to the *Isleworthian* magazine.

Even a thicko like Vortimer Williams knew what that meant; it was from one of the immensely rare (and presumably valuable) 'double-black' packs printed by Thomas De La Rue and Sons for Queen Victoria after the death of the Prince Consort in 1861. One fawning contemporary remarked, 'As day turned to perpetual night, the Queen turned to solitaire, and even the hearts and diamonds wore mourning dress.'[130] And who did Gray know who owned not one pack but several, some unopened? Why, Merlin of course, whose mother was a De La Rue and a direct descendant of the founder of that august printing establishment. It was no secret – many of the teaching staff had played poker at Merlin's. He was a very good player and even wrote a poker column for a respected periodical[131] – a sort of large, elderly, male Victoria Coren. As a disinterested observer, I would have to say that he was less attractive. He would frequently host games which were attended by the great and the good of Isleworth academia – Gray excepted as, according to him, he is completely incapable of deception. In any case, card games bore him.

As far as Gray knew, the only other double-black cards were at Osborne House, Queen Victoria's Italianate villa on the Isle of Wight. Other than Swoboda's Indian portraits, Gray considered the cards the only conceivable reason to visit that wretched mausoleum. So the card would obviously make the plods think of Merlin, although it would not certainly constitute any sort of proof. Not that he imagined Vortimer Williams would worry much about proof.

The poison, of course, would tend to implicate Merlin – an obscure botanical toxin would be right up his street – at least, it would be if he developed a homicidal streak. The note, unless in his handwriting, was meaningless, but the card...

---

130   Sir Hugh Wintlesham, *A Courtier's Tale,* Chatto, 1901.
131   I think it might have been *Intelligence and National Security,* or the *Bodleian Library Record.*

Merlin returned looking as though he were anticipating a week or two on the Côte d'Azure rather than detention in the campus clink. He did actually confirm to me at a later date that, hellish though the Isleworth cells were, he did actually consider them preferable to the Côte d'Azure. He winked pantomimically and slapped Gray on the shoulder (a well-meant gesture which almost felled him). 'Well, I'll be off, Gerrish,' he said.

Gray made to accompany him but was informed by Haddow that his attendance would be 'unnecessary'. and by Harris that it would be 'inconducive to the public good'. When Merlin echoed the sentiment, he took the hint: 'Well, see you soon. I'll find out who did it, Merlin.'

'Oh, I'm not worrying, Gerrish,' he smiled; 'You should concentrate on the Madonna. Yllingstone's the key, I think.'

It was only then that Gray wondered if there were a connection between the Madonna and the murder. Could it be a coincidence that the body turned up right next to the fake Madonna just as they were investigating the disappearance of the original? The first murder on the University's grounds since the Golden Twins case in the 1930s and the first ever disappearance of a painting from the Snakenborg Collection were surely linked. If there were a connection, Yllingstone could be the key to both cases. But Yllingstone couldn't help Gray – he was off his chump, as those few of us unafflicted by political correctness say. Nonetheless, there was something about Yllingstone which had been nagging Gray since he had been to see him. There was something, but he was damned if he could fathom what it was.

He did what any self-respecting member of the University would do in such circumstances, he became an owl. As the evening was drawing in, you may even say that he became a night owl. There is a certain magic in sandstone colonnades at dusk, although, as an owl, you had to be rather careful which order of architecture you adopted. As observed by Sir John Soane in 1777 (though not quite in these terms), for straight-forward pondering, such as what to have for supper or which horse to back in the 2.40, Ionic columns, especially unfluted ones, are to be preferred (or, at a pinch Doric, which always have fluted shafts). The simplicity of the Doric order engages right brain activity and is conducive to quick decision-making. Ionic columns, even if unfluted, move the mental processes up a notch, switching some activity to the left brain. But Ionic columns, while fine for everyday intellectual analysis, are of limited use for truly creative problem-solving; for this only Corinthian columns with fluted shafts are really suitable. The entablature is usually disregarded when assessing a colonnade's suitability for owling, although simplicity of the architrave and frieze is desirable, as is only modest ornamentation of the cornice. I need hardly say that the material from which the columns are constructed is also of the utmost importance, but it is a much more subjective matter than the architectural order. Gray, a conservative man at heart, favoured various sandstones, although limestone, particularly Portland stone, was not to be despised.[132] Wooden columns, as they are not commonly to be found in quadrangles or any other extramural environment, are irrelevant to both the owl and the scobolotcher, but Gray knew of more than one Old Etonian who ascribed his success in later life to the years he spent in the shadow of the wooden Corinthian columns of the college's exquisite library. The collonading on the north side of Isleworth's Em Quad (the only side to have a colonnade) is Ionic, but, fortunately for Gray, that of Bleeding Heart Quad is Corinthian, and of Cotswold sandstone, so it was there that he owled away the hours. There was a lurking danger in Bleeding Heart Quad, but we shall come that anon.

Back to Gray's musings: if he couldn't get anything out of Yllingstone himself, perhaps he should look into his background. It

---

132   Here is not the place to discuss the subtleties of owling. I have not even touched upon the virtues (and vices) of the Composite and Solomonic orders, nor the alarming growth in pilaster-based cogitation in the eighteenth century. For all these, the reader is advised to await Professor Gray's forthcoming book, provisionally entitled *The Lay Person's Guide to Owling*. One can only hope that it appears more swiftly than his monograph on the letter K.

seemed unlikely he was a career criminal – most gallery directors, in his limited experience, were not[133] – but perhaps he had a gambling habit or was being blackmailed over strange peccadilloes. Anything which might encourage him to steal a valuable painting. The university archives would be no use – even if they contained his personnel files, those would be sealed, and would they really contain anything revealing in any case? Gray could try Mrs Yllingstone, but he didn't think that would do him much good. What was it about Yllingstone? There was something nagging at the back of his mind that even the finest Corinthian columns could not dislodge. He decided to visit him again, however useless it seemed.

It was Gray's misfortune, while his unwary mind was in its wonted higher plane, to encounter the aforementioned lurking danger. It is an unfortunate accident of history... but I shall not bore you with history, especially since you can so easily look it up in the Annals.[134] Suffice it to say that since the Second Battle of Turnham Green on 13 November 1642 the Vice-Chancellor,[135] as Master of the Bleeding Heart, has always officially resided in Bleeding Heart Quad, the unfortunate corollary of which being that, at the time in question, that academical perturbatrix, Dr Millicent Behr, also resided therein and at this moment appeared silently among the shadows. No ghost in a revenge tragedy, nor ghoul, nor monk in a gothic horror could be a less welcome apparition to Professor Gray at that moment than this golden-haired harpy. I may, or may not, have previously adverted to the fact that Gray's experience of women was, despite (or perhaps because of) a brief period of matrimo-

---

133 Though some, especially the art historians (according to Gray) among them, are less than scrupulous.

134 Anon, *Annals of the Moſt Antient University of Isleworth in the County of Middle-sex from the earlieſt times unto the reign of His Most Excellent Maiesty King Charles the second. and including A Charter of King Canute written in the Saxon tongue,* Syon: Printed and Sold by J. G. at the signe of the Bleeding Heart MDCLXXXIII, p. 468.

135 At that time, Prince Rupert. It is to John Aubrey, in his *Brief Lives,* that we owe the explanation of why, ever since 1642, the roles of Vice-Chancellor and Master of the Bleeding Heart have been combined. Unfortunately, the relevant passage is usually omitted from the printed editions. See his life of Ithamara Reginalds, Oxford: Bodleian Library MS. Aubrey 23A, ff. 13 v–15 r.

ny, both limited and less than entirely positive. This is, no doubt, regrettable, and I believe he does regret it, but there are some women, however great their physical attractions (or perhaps because of them), whose predatory instincts fill him with dread, especially when he seems to be their favoured prey (so he tells me). Since the demise of Millicent's brief fling with Merlin (apparently she'd left him for a cosmologist, a rocket-scientist or something equally absurd), it appeared (at least to the man himself) that Gray had been elevated to flavour of the month.

It has been admitted, by wiser men than either me or Professor Gray, that Dr Millicent Behr was far from unattractive. Indeed, that was part of the problem. Unchivalrous as it may seem, Gray believed that he could, should the occasion arise, resist the blandishments of an ugly woman by being brusque or even rude. But the occasion had not arisen and Millicent was not ugly. Without wishing to discuss, *inter alia*, Adelard of Bath's assertion that a light and fiery air travels out from the brain, through the optic nerves and then, having received an impression of some external object, makes the return journey, Gray had to admit that Millicent had what seemed to be quite literally piercing eyes.[136] He couldn't swear to their colour, especially in the present crepuscular light; sometimes in the past they had seemed blue, sometimes green and occasionally black. In the half-light, shaded by a column (of the Corinthian order), the whites shined out and the irises looked merely black; in fact (*pace* Adelard, this is a rods and cones thing) she appeared entirely monochrome which, as was the case with many a screen goddess of the thirties, lent her a sculptural beauty. He wondered in passing, and in some obscure region of his brain which was disengaged from the fight-or-flight impulse, if the introduction of colour film had destroyed as many cinematic careers as the advent of sound.

---

136 Readers seeking a wider understanding of the relationship between medieval optical theory, love-sickness and lust are recommended to read Jacqueline Tasioulas, ' "Dying of imagination" in the first fragment of the *Canterbury Tales*,' *Medium Aevum*, lxxxii (2), 2013, pp. 213–235.

'Hello, Gerrish,' she purred with some of the expectant throati-ness of a tigress about to sink her teeth into the tasty rump of a suc-culent (and excessively naïve) young gazelle. In the open he could outrun her, but here, at the very entrance to her lair, he was trapped.

'Millicent, what a pleasant surprise.'

'Have you been avoiding me?' she asked with unalluring play-fulness.

'Of course not,' he replied and, with a touch of the Gerrish Gray quick thinking which so often got him into trouble, 'I'm here, ar-en't I? I'd hardly hide from you, just outside your l... er, lodgings.'

'We call it a house, darling. "Lodgings" sounds so squalid, doesn't it? Come in and have a drink. You can tell me what you were doing lurking outside. I've often wondered if you were a peeping tom.' She didn't sound disapproving at this preposterous suggestion and Gray was more surprised than ever that Merlin had ever chosen to spend time with the woman whom he sometimes referred to as 'the daughter of Hippocrates'. Gray couldn't quite place the reference.

Needless to say, the Snakenborg Professor of Cultural History acquiesced, but reluctantly as he knew that the Master of the Bleed-ing Heart was at a conference on the future of Higher Education in Chennai, and Millicent would have him to herself. The Master's House, which slots more-or-less into the northeast corner of the quad, is an elegant affair by Inigo Jones, completed in 1618, while he was still working on the Banqueting House in Whitehall. When they were digging the foundations they found part of a bronze Ro-man breastplate for an elephant, perhaps the very one which (ac-cording to Polyænus in his Στρατηγήματα) Julius Cæsar used to overcome King Cassivellaunus's defences at the Battle of Brentford in 54 B.C. After all, how many elephant breastplates of that period have ever been found in Isleworth or thereabouts?[137]

Unfortunately, the interior of the Master's House bore all the marks of a professional interior decorator, striving to be differ-

---

137 I cannot confidently answer this question, which you may regard as rhetorical, but it is reasonable to believe that there have not been many.

ent while showing no spark of originality, rather like the annual tomfoolery of the Turner Prize. There were sofas with plump satin-clad cushions which had never borne the impress of head, back or buttocks, curtains which had been ruched or swagged within an inch of their lives (it's curtains for you, Bugsy), contrasting with harsh glass and metal surfaces, sunken spotlights, sixties-style plastic chairs in colours more primal-scream than primary. The walls (some white, some lilac) were covered with large, abstract daubs in lifeless metal frames. Fitted carpets shouted, 'Look at me; I'm oatmeal with a hint of lavender (10% polyamide).' Gray wondered what English Heritage had been doing when this Grade I building had been thus desecrated, although it was doubtful if their writ ran as far Isleworth.

Perhaps to avoid the carpets, Gray looked at Millicent and, rather unwisely, at her eyes – despite the spotlights, they were still as black as treacle and as hard as titanium nitride. He'd have felt more at ease dining with the Borgias or looking down from the guillotine at Madame Defarge with her tricotage (though all the most discerning critics agree that the French have never excelled at knitwear). At last he fully understood how Johnny must have felt in the presence of Fanny Cradock.

She mixed him a gimlet and made herself something vile with grenadine – is there anything which isn't vile to be made with grenadine? Mercifully the gimlet was made from an admixture of both Waitrose's lime cordial and fresh lime juice with Plymouth gin – he'd once had an unfortunate encounter with Bombay Sapphire, an innately tarty drink unsuited to the serious tippler.

She wasn't wearing very much and what there was clung for dear life to the curves. Dangerous curves, as Peter Cheyney would have said.

It is time to draw a dicsreet veil over the proceedings. I have no wish to pry and, of course, I wasn't there.

16: Twickenham by Moonlight

There is not so untittletattling a village as Twickenham in the island.[138]

GRAY WOKE UP the next morning – oh, you want to know what happened the night before? But this is neither the time nor the place. In any case, as I have already said, I was not there. Originally, he would tell me no more than that he woke up in his own bed suffering from a headache. He told me that Pugwash would have thrown a wobbly had he not returned to feed him.

Later, he came clean, although (to my relief) he went into no details. Millicents's advances which, under normal circumstances, could only be described as irresistible in the same way that the advance of a Panzer division might be, were to no avail because he had a prior engagement that evening at Twickenham Studios.

If you had the idea that there was something glamorous about film studios, thought Gray (an idea which he had never entertained himself), a visit to Twickenham Studios would surely disabuse you. Not that he thought they *should* be glamorous, any more than a film star should be glamorous off-screen. These days, of course, the poor dears couldn't even manage to be glamorous in front of the camera. This particular studio, crammed into an undistinguished suburban street close to St Margaret's railway station, consisted of a few shabby, low-rise buildings. Presumably, at the time of the Snakenborg Gallery's leaking roof, they offered the promise of a more secure and weatherproof storage space than any which could be afforded within the campus. For all Gray knew, they still did.

Dismounting from his Brompton and stowing his bicycle clips in a jacket pocket, Gray was greeted by the implausibly named Bella Toye, who led him through a maze of shabby passages.

---

138   Horace Walpole quoted in *The Letters of Thomas Gray,* Duncan C. Tovey ed., London: G. Bell and sons, 1900, vol. II, p. 92

'I'm afraid we seem to have binned all our storage records from the early seventies,' she said as she strode ahead of him, 'so I thought you ought to meet Old Ted. He's the only person left who was around at the time, and he says he remembers the paintings.'

Old Ted's lair was a small and littered cubicle, little bigger than a night watchman's hut, and Old Ted filled it rather amply. Indeed, his bulk was such that, given free rein, it looked as though it could fill the Albert Hall. His skin had the sponginess and puffy resilience of an unbaked loaf; he looked like nothing so much as the Pillsbury Doughboy grown old and weary, and very, very fat.

He smiled, 'Fergive me if I don't stand up,' he said; 'I'm not as young as I was. Funny, that, actually. They used to call me Young Ted in those days, back in the seventies. Then one day – it must've been about 1985 – they started calling me Old Ted. I was only about thirty-five fer chrissake! They never called me just Ted. One day I was Young and the next day I was Old. Old before me time I was.'

'Well, I'll leave you to it,' said Miss Toye, evidently glad to escape what was probably a much-rehearsed complaint.

'Tata, doll,' said Old Ted to her retreating figure. She's alright,' he added.

'You remember when the paintings from Isleworth University were put into storage?' Gray prompted.

'Course I do, mate. I was Young Ted then. Didn't 'ave much of a heducation – secondary modern – but I was into what you'd call fine art in those days and that Mr Hyllingstone 'ad some luverly paintings – nudes an' stuff – in an artistic way of course. Didn't like the religious stuff much, though. You know the sort of thing – some geezer wiv a lotta arrows in him, a miserable-looking cow wiv an annoying brat in her hands, that sorta thing. One or two were OK, I suppose, but give me a naked bird any day, as long as it's art, you know, not smut.'

'Quite. I wonder if you remember this picture?' Gray handed him a postcard of the Isleworth Madonna. 'The picture itself is about three feet tall and two wide, in a very large, ornate gilt frame.'

'Too right I do. Nearly did my back in lifting her. You wouldn't believe how heavy that frame is. Painting itself's pretty heavy, too. Painted on a solid plank of wood, and not light wood like balsa, somethin' 'eavy.'

That startled Gray. 'You took it out of the frame?'

'Yeah. Hyllingstone asked me to, fer the uvver geezer. Couldn't get it in 'is car else. Very small car. Brought the painting back a couple of months later and I put it back in the frame.'

'I see. Do you know who the other man was?'

'I didn't at the time.'

'But you do now?'

'Course I do. Seen 'im on the telly. Balding, white beard, smoked like a chimney. It was that Keating bloke what painted them Samuel Palmers. Not that they looked like Palmers to me. They 'ad sheep in 'em but that was all the resemblance. I've seem them ones in the Ash-mooly-ann. Don't reckon he 'ad or he'd a done a better job.'

Well, well. The notorious art forger, Tom Keating had taken away the Madonna.

'Haven't thought about that picture in years. 'Sfunny axially. There was another person askin' 'bout it th'other day. Ugly bint with orange 'air', skin the colour of yeller hochre.'

17: Painting by Numbers

The whole notion of individual genius and lone enterprise in the Italian Renaissance is belied by both the co-operative nature of workshop production and the technical complexities of the finished products themselves.[139]

WHEN GRAY GOT back to his house, the telephone was ringing. It was Tim Hutchisson. He was panting like an enthusiastic gun-dog presenting his grateful owner with a mouthful of pheasant: 'OK, I won't bore you with the details. We couldn't use dendrochonology on the panel – taking the sample would have destroyed the painting. However, there is nothing untoward there; it is poplar, with a gesso ground which we identified by XRD as being calcium sulphate dihydrate (gypsum to you). The *imprimitura,* composed of powdered glass, white lead and a dash of lead–tin yellow, is consistent with Raphael's usual materials. Infrared reflectography revealed metalpoint underdrawing which is detailed and masterly. There are signs of pouncing, indicating that the main outlines were transferred from a pricked cartoon. Fourier transform infrared spectroscopy and gas chromatography–mass spectroscopy show the binding material of the pigments to be walnut oil. All the pigments and the binder in the main body of the painting are those which would have been available in Raphael's time.'

Gray could feel his brain spinning down like an inactive hard disk, but he didn't interrupt, for fear the art historian would start again from the beginning. In any case, he thought it was good to give one's brain a rest. It reduced the number of calories one burnt and thus, some would no doubt have one believe, save the planet.

---

139   Ross King, 'Painting by Numbers: Was the Sistine Chapel the Work of a Lone Genius, or the Collaborative Effort of Bickering Apprentices?' *New Statesman,* 25 November 2002.

'My own opinion, for what it's worth…' [If only he knew how little Gray valued the opinions of art historians!] 'is that the brushwork looks authentic and that the painting just looks right. But back to the scientific analysis – the pigments and binder used in painting the Crystal Palace transmitter are also consistent with the early sixteenth century, although the subject matter is clearly not. However, the underdrawing shows what appears to be a wooden tower in the same position. There are some signs of this having been painted and then erased, probably during the original painting. By the way, there is substantial evidence of water damage. It looks fairly recent – say the last fifty years.'

'Aha,' Gray said.

'Yes. I'll have our van driver bring the painting back tomorrow.'

'Oh, no, don't do that,' the Professor replied; 'I have a plan. Not a word to anyone.' It was a glorious and gloriously simple plan. He didn't have to do a thing, which was, almost by definition, the ideal sort of plan. He did not advocate indolence, *per se;* it was simply that the less one did, the fewer mistakes one made. Even quite clever people make the mistake of – well, being too clever and making mistakes. Consider the case of those who plotted the death of Alexander Litvinenko, not by pushing him under a bus, but poisoning him with polonium, an element so rare that the trail, quite literally led back to Moscow. Conservation of energy, also (as he had previously remarked), was not to be despised.

In the 𝕸atter of the 𝕸adonna, everything was very satisfactory. At least, it seemed that way to him at that moment. It was now time to turn his mind back to the dead body in the Snakenborg Gallery, time to talk to Yllingstone again.

18: The Meadows

... Nature the goddess
Wole of hir oughne fre largesse
With herbes and with floures bothe
The feldes and the medwes clothe.'[140]

THE MEADOWS WAS as attractive and welcoming as he remembered it. It didn't look (easy-clean surfaces), smell (disinfectant, boiled cabbage) or sound (wailing, over-loud televisions) in any way institutional. Despite the editorial in *Investor's Business Daily*,[141] Gray didn't arrive there concerned about Yllingstone's welfare in the hands of Britain's 'evil and Orwellian' National Health Service. As it turned out, his confidence in Yllingstone's long-term health was unfounded.

The former curator was ensconced in a large armchair with the *Daily Telegraph* upside-down in front of him. His face was grey and blank, although his eyes flitted back and forth, hesitantly right to left, then quickly left to right.

'We have to talk,' Gray said, yanking him up by his wrist and guiding him to a table on the terrace. There was a cool breeze and there was no-one else around. 'It's quite clear that there is nothing wrong with you, Mr Yllingstone,' he continued as they sat down.

The former curator gazed down and moved his lips but no sound came out. He cleared his throat and it occurred to Gray that this was possibly the first time he'd tried to speak in years and he was having to relearn the technique. Eventually he began, speaking softly without looking up: 'How did you know?'

---

140   John Gower, *Confessio Amantis,* lines 55961–4.
141   31 July 2009: 'People such as scientist Stephen Hawking wouldn't have a chance in the U.K., where the National Health Service would say the life of this brilliant man, because of his physical handicaps, is essentially worthless.'

'I was willing to believe that someone suffering from dementia could initially be misdiagnosed as suffering a nervous breakdown – I'm told it does happen – but I couldn't believe that a man with dementia would consistently hold the *Daily Telegraph* upside-down in front of him. Your cognitive skills were clearly sufficient to select the same newspaper every day. That could just indicate a preference for a particular size and colour, the only other national daily broadsheet being the *Financial Times,* which is a revolting shade of salmon pink. Perhaps you disliked pink. But holding it upside down every day showed that you could recognise which way up it was. The obvious conclusion – and I'm a great enthusiast for the obvious – was that you were reading it upside down, hardly a sign of serious mental impairment. The lateral movement of your eyes confirmed my surmise; reading upside-down, so from right to left at reading speed and then swiftly back to the right for the line above it. You started at the bottom of the page and moved up, which is to say, from the beginning of the article to the end. I also noticed that you tended to have the paper open at the business section. What I can't understand is why.'

'Do I really have to explain why I read business section of the *Telegraph*?' asked Yllingstone, getting into his stride; 'I do, as it happens, favour a broadsheet paper, I don't particularly like salmon pink and, as a Conservative, I find the general tenor of the *Telegraph* to my liking and since even that paper is now infested with celebrities and fashion, I read the business section which is reasonably free of both.'

'You know what I mean. Why are you here?'

'It's a long story,' he said with a sigh, 'and I'm not sure that it's any of your business.'

'Oh, it is very much my business, Mr Yllingstone. My name is Gerrish Gray and I'm the Snakenborg Professor. You will appreciate that my career is intimately bound up with the Snakenborg Collection.'

Yllingstone sighed again and Gray feared that he would relapse into his customary silence, but at last he spoke again: 'I really am not well, Professor Gray. My nervous breakdown was quite genuine, though short-lived, and I have two illnesses that only death will cure – I am a compulsive gambler and an alcoholic.'

'But why pretend to be gaga? Why are you here?'

'Gambling, which can certainly be regarded as a mental illness in my case, was my downfall – that and the leaking roof. You've heard of the Tweezle brother, I expect?' he asked but Gray never had the opportunity to reply. Above the moan of doves, not in elms which had proved less than immemorial due to fungal disease, but in ancient oaks and beeches, he barely felt the air whiffle near his cheek and a fountain of red appeared from Yllingstone's neck. Simultaneously, or so it seemed, Gray heard a crack behind him, perhaps from the bushes on the boundary of the property. In an instant the former curator's alcoholism, gambling addiction and feigned dementia were cured. Yllingstone was dead – someone had shot him dead. Gray scuttled inside in case someone wanted to take a pot at him too. Even as a universal panacea, death held no allure.

A resident doctor, a fussy little man with a ginger comb-over and a tired expression, braved the terrace to examine Yllingstone, although he was clearly dead, while the receptionist called an unavailing ambulance and the police – the Metropolitan kind not the University's Mickey Mouse variety,[142] for they were well outside the Isleworth campus.

Gray realised that, as he had been with Yllingstone when he died, he was probably a suspect and was certainly a witness so he had no choice but to hang around. Given how close the bullet had passed him, it was even possible that he had been the intended victim.

---

142 Why the term Mickey Mouse should be used pejoratively, is a matter of hot contention in the Senior Common Rooms and cloistered snugnesses of Isleworth.

19: Bluebottles

I will have you as soundly swindgd for this, you blew-Bottel'd rogue.[143]

In Isleworth on a bench I ate
A Keens's Black with no regret
For all the tumult there had been
Upon the famous cricket green,
Where, long before the sun had set,
The gentlemen and players met.
Estates and fortunes both were bet
On the match like none e'er seen
In Isleworth.[144]

WITHIN A SURPRISINGLY short time, uniformed police officers had arrived – not, mercifully, Isleworth Bulls but real ones from the Metropolitan Police. They buzzed around energetically if ineffectually, conforming to the old-fashioned soubriquet 'bluebottles'. Professor Gray was mulling over the various words for officers of the law – plods, Peelers, cops, rozzers, the fuzz, the Bill, and many less endearing terms – when his revery was interrupted by a very different sort of policeman. From his clothes to his voice, he was the very reincarnation of those solid, tweedy detectives played by the likes of John McCallum (I'm thinking of his *Long Memory* phase rather than his *Skippy the Bush Kangaroo* phase) or Jack Hawkins in countless old British films. When he spoke, it was with the same gravelly tones and quiet authority as Gideon of the Yard, and it was with difficul-

---

143   Shakespeare, *Henry IV,* pt II, v. iv. 20.
144   W. E. Henley's unfinished rondeau bears clear similarities to his 'In Rotten Row'. The significance of Keens's Black will become apparent later. The attention of younger readers is drawn to the rhyming of *ate* with *regret*. This once-standard British pronunciation of ate seems to have been foolishly discarded in recent years causing much inconvenience to the poetic classes.

ty that Gray suppressed the desire to tell him he'd been at Twicken-ham Studios the night before; and surely this stern official would have been neither amused nor interested.

Flanked by a plain-clothes sergeant of impressive girth and a spindly constable, the tweed-clad detective pulled out his note-book with a flourish; 'Chief Inspector Clanarsh, and you are sir?'

'Gerrish Gray.'

'And what were you doing, visiting the deceased, sir? Are you a relation?'

Gray told him of his investigations into the missing Isleworth Madonna and the fact that Yllingstone was entirely *compos mentis*, merely in hiding from the forces of disorder.

'The Tweezle brothers, eh,' said Clanarsh. 'My uncle Huggon was in the Force and he was always talking about them. A very nasty class of villain by all accounts, local lads who fancied they were West London's answer to the Krays. They were quite ambitious, even had links with the Triads in Hong Kong. But Ray died in about 1990 and Gerald retired to the Costa del Crime before I made sergeant. Mr Yllingstone could have safely left here years ago.'

'I think he was quite happy here.'

'Surprisingly comfortable,' sniffed Clanarsh, 'but you couldn't drag me in here. So, sir, any idea why anyone would want to kill him? I can't see someone killing over a picture stolen decades ago, however valuable.'

Gray, while not entirely agreeing with the inspector, could offer no suggestions and, having assured the detective that he would not leave the area without letting him know and accepting his card, he remounted his Brompton and headed back to Isleworth. The gen-eral miasma of depression which engulfed him was exacerbated by a steady grey drizzle which grew heavier as the the wind got up. Stray blasts of cool air reminded him of the perturbation of the air he had felt when Yllingstone was shot. Now, he almost imagined that every breeze signified a rifle shot aimed at him. And *that* prompted another uncomfortable question: had the shot been aimed at Yllingstone or Gray himself? As Clanarsh had suggested, it seemed far-fetched that anyone would kill the former curator over the ancient theft of the Madonna. On the other hand, there seemed even less motive for wishing to murder Gray. He knew absolutely *nothing*, as Merlin was fond of reminding him.

It was in this melancholy frame of mind that Gray shot, rather too fast, through Isleworth's venerable north-east gateway (honeyed sandstone, greyed in places by excessive weathering), narrowly missing the almost equally venerable and weathered porter who shouted 'oi!' and raised a clenched fist to the errant academic, although whether he recognised the motion-blurred cyclist as the Snakenborg Professor is open to question. Had he, surely deference to the great man would have stayed his hand. Gray, sweating like the proverbial pig (do pigs sweat?), eased on the brakes and thrust out his feet to bring the bicycle to a juddering halt before it could hit the unforgiving cobbles (after gravel, a Brompton's most relentless foe) of Vast Quad. He looked around; it was an area of the campus which he usually avoided, not least because it included within its massy walls of ashlared sandstone the execrable Ivo Penn-Westerman LLD, Professor of Theology. Unbidden by celestial powers and, even more certainly, by Gerrish Gray, a small, balding man with a perpetual smile emerged from a door way shouting, 'Morning, Gerrish!'

'Morning, Ivo, aren't you supposed to be in church?'

The usual rebuke had Penn-Westerman chuckling; 'It is not by blindly following the ancient rituals that we best serve God, as I'm sure you know, Gerrish. I'm off to a meeting of the St Kew Missionary Society to snatch a million souls from the jaws of hell,' referring to a charity of which Penn-Westerman was a trustee. Although nominally financing St Kew's Mission in northern Pakistan, almost everyone but Penn-Westerman was aware that the society was being investigated by the Charity Commission and the security forces of several countries on suspicion of using its funds to promote a world-wide jihad against all non-muslims, not to mention shiites and most muslims who did not agree with the Salafist agenda of those who managed its funds.

Gray had once attempted to draw this to Penn-Westerman's attention and had been forced to listen to a long lecture on Christian tolerance as his reward. By St Petroc, he would get even with His Smarminess, but for the moment the Snakenborg Professor smiled and waved to Penn-Westerman as he pushed his Brompton towards the the small passage which led from Vast Quad to Cricket Field Lane and King Arthur's Grave, a small, grassy mound surrounded by scrub and shady trees. The mound had been excavated in Victorian times, in the usual slapdash manner of the period, yielding nothing more exciting than a few medieval bottles, believed to have once held Rhenish wines of inferior quality. No-one had ever discovered evidence for a cricket pitch in the vicinity, although the game was known to have been popular at the University in the seventeenth century, even to the exclusion of cock-fighting. Both were reprobated by Statute of the University's Yearly Council[145] in 1649, although only cricket was officially banned from University property. When cricket was finally permitted to return, after the Restoration, it was only on the strict understanding that overs consisted of five balls rather then the four then favoured throughout the rest of the realm. I digress, but it is not unreasonable to suppose (and indeed he assures me that this was the case) that Gray's mind was occupied with thoughts of Rhenish wine and missing cricket pitches as he made his way back to his rooms. If he recited W. E. Henley's famous rondeau at the same time, I should not be entirely surprised. There were, it is true, two dead bodies to claim his attention but they were not so clearly within the remit of the Snakenborg Professor of Cultural History.

The only disadvantage of taking this shorter route from northeast to south-west, apart from the encounter with Penn-Wester-

---

145 It is a reflection of Isleworth's preference for both plain English words and minimal governance that it has always chosen to regulate itself on a yearly rather than hebdomodal basis.

man, was that the narrow lanes were restricted to pedestrian traffic, forcing Gray to either break the ancient bye-laws or wheel his bike along the tortuous route. As a pillar of the establishment, the Snakenborg Professor naturally chose the former option, although the wobbling which restricted lateral movement and a stream of oncoming pedestrians inflicted upon the venerable person and his Brompton was probably far more demanding than either pushing his bicycle or cycling around the perimeter of the campus to the south-west gate. In any case, Gray had little time to consider such things, his mind being occupied by Rhenish wine and cricket pitches, and possibly also gunmen, corpses, paintings and Merlin, festering away (as he imagined) in Isleworth University clink. He made a mental note to check the derivation of 'clink'. Was it a reference to the the shutting of cell doors or the sound of manacles and leg irons, once so popular with the English penal system, and still in vogue with that of the United States of America? As so often, Gray had found that the fierce intellectual rigour which he had brought to the Madonna, the body in the gallery and the death of Yllingstone had somehow been dissipated by consideration of lesser matters. Perhaps he suffered from attention deficit disorder; there was, undoubtedly, a meandering nature to his mind. No doubt the origin of 'clink' was important but it could wait for examination another time. With that resolved *pro tem,* his mind naturally slipped back into the history of Cricket at Isleworth, a subject in which he had only an academic interest, since he had little idea how the game was played; he remembered seeing white-clad figures disporting themselves in a rather leisurely fashion on a strip of green which he took to be the current cricket pitch but what they were doing and how they scored the game were still something of a mystery to him. Had he an inclination to take up any sport, he felt, it would be one like that, in which most of the participants stood still (or so it seemed) for several hours at a time. His rules on the conservation of energy were ever to the fore.

Thus it was, intellectually refreshed but no nearer solving either murder and having only partly resolved, he felt, the matter of the Isleworth Madonna, that Professor Gray arrived back at his rooms. It was only after he had hauled his Brompton up the treacherous and winding oak staircase that he questioned whether such activity accorded with his distaste for exercise. Slumping into the somewhat limp embrace of an overstuffed armchair the leather of which had seen better days, and many of them, the Great Man finally turned his mind again to the Madonna and the murders. It seemed most improbable that the three were not connected, and yet the question of the Madonna was more-or-less solved to his satisfaction and he was uncertain if it shed any light on either murder. It might help if he knew who the first victim was, something which Merlin could tell him, he was sure.

If his interpretation of the mystery surrounding the Madonna was correct, it was hard to see how anyone could gain from killing Yllingstone. Perhaps, therefore, his supposed solution was wrong. Perhaps some interested party had stolen the Madonna, or appeared to steal it, for a more devious reason. The Isleworth Madonna was worth many millions but nothing compared with the whole Snakenborg Collection, which would all go to Marietta and Esther if the terms of the will were breached. But if that had been the intention, Marietta and Esther were too young to have been involved and why hadn't the family made any move to reveal the phoney Madonna before? As far as he could see, this idea was a dead end, although it might explain the killing of Yllingstone. He felt muddled and decided he should speak to Merlin as soon as possible. Despite the doubtful benefits of consuming various herbal concoctions, the Emeritus Professor of Chemistry had a mind as sharp as a pin. Gray, having effectively delegated the solution of the crimes to his imprisoned colleague, thought he deserved a glass or two of Saint-Estèphe, which he duly consumed while listening to some Handel, by which treatment the furrows in his brow were gently ironed out and his mind returned to its natural equilibrium.

He observed with growing fascination a speck of dust caught in the light from the large leaded windows, darting here and there as the turbulence of convection currents diverted it from its proper, gravity-enforced path towards the carpet. Who knew how many hours it would take to descend? Perhaps, he thought, it would never land, caught in a purgatory of Brownian motion (although this term sounded vaguely gastroenterological to Gray).

Before dropping off for a brief siesta, the Snakenborg Professor decided to visit Merlin in gaol later that afternoon to see if he could help him in his investigations. Alas! It was not to be.

20: The Strange Case of the Poorly Professor

Be careful about reading health books. You may die of a misprint.[146]

GRAY AMBLED IN the sunshine, as only a more-or-less-tenured professor at a leading university can amble, with quiet assurance and no sense of purpose, to the handsome Georgian sandstone building which contained both the University Police Station and the gaol, known variously as the Clink, Pokey or, perhaps more accurately reflecting the quality of the accommodation, the Black Hole.[147] It had been a pleasant and uneventful stroll which little prepared him for the news which awaited for him.

'I'm sorry, sir,' said Sergeant Quayle at the desk, 'Professor Le-Maistre has been rushed to hospital.'

Gray was stunned. Merlin was the healthiest man he knew. 'What is it?' he asked.

'They say, sir, that it is acute nutmeg poisoning, although they,' he directed his eyes upward to the Proctor's office, 'don't know their arse from their elbow. Why, I probably drink more nutmeg cola than the professor and I've never been so well in my life.'

Quayle's immense girth and violently puce complexion did not really seem to add credence to this assertion, but Gray nodded in agreement, perhaps remembering the twenty-one stone weakling which Quayle had once been. 'The University Hospital, I take it?'

'Aye.'

---

146 Mark Twain.
147 'Of Calcutta' being understood but never spoken. There is a persistent rumour that the cells were actually modelled on survivors' reports but this is clearly impossible since they predate the event by more than fifty years. It seems, in fact, that the cells only declined into their present state when the Brawling Act of 1551 (which had brought in many fines of £5 for disorderly behaviour on church property) was superseded by the Ecclesiastical Courts Jurisdiction Act of 1860.

This was hardly surprising. With a large clientele of students (and particularly student doctors), the hospital had almost unrivalled expertise in the areas of toxicology and chemical dependency. Gray made his way to the hospital with an urgency and sense of purpose which had been signally lacking from his previous demeanour, stopping at Merlin's garden to pick some Black Isleworth strawberries.

The large, modern, gleaming white structure dominated the Shallows. It had none of the antiquated charm of the old Isleworth Royal Infirmary, which was in the process of conversion into a vast student union complex, but it probably offered less cosy accommodation to pathogens as well. On balance, Gray thought he would prefer to be patient in the new building but a student in the old. He was relieved, on enquiring at reception to learn that Merlin was well enough to receive visitors. He caught the lift to the fifth floor.

Merlin was not a small man, six foot four and built for caber tossing rather than hurdles, so Gray was shocked to find him almost hidden by the rather skimpy hospital bed linen, a small face peeking out from a sea of white like the bedraggled sole survivor of a torpedoed merchantman tossed upon spumy seas. His black hair had turned overnight to grey with streaks of white. Around him were arrayed great swags of tubes, cables and drips. Polychromatic monitors flashed and beeped and buzzed to no discernible tune or purpose. Gray wondered if he had been relying on his friend too much. Surely the Snakenborg Professor could resolve the case without the aid of this broken man? Merlin slipped a hand from under the sheets and silently beckoned him forward. 'Hah! Gerrish! Good to see you,' he said and his tone was almost hearty.

'How are you?' Gray asked.

'Me? I'm fine, of course. Oh, I see what you mean. It was a bit dull in the clink and the food is indescribably vile. Not that it's much good here, but at least friends can bring me fruit, as I see you have. I don't suppose you brought a single malt? Never mind. Next time, eh?'

'So you're not ill.'

'Oh no. Not at all. I faked a few convulsions but I didn't really expect them to fall for it. Those chumps wouldn't know nutmeg poisoning from a hole in the head. You know, there are almost no reported cases of myristicin poisoning and, of course, they require the ingestion of nutmeg – and rather a lot of it at that – and I can tell you there is absolutely none in the prison diet. Where did they think I was getting it from? Smuggled in by some well-meaning friend like you, perhaps. Anyway, how's the investigation going? Mind you, the Vice-Chancellor has just come back from the far east and he and Millicent brought me a few bottles of nutmeg cola.'

The Snakenborg Professor told him about the results of the scientific analysis of the painting, his visit to Twickenham Studios, and Yllingstone's death.

'Dear, dear,' said Merlin, 'It is really turning from a comic opera into a tragic third act, with more than a hint of shaggy dog story to boot.' And his friend didn't disagree, although the comic aspect had eluded him.

'I hear,' the grizzled eminence of the Chemistry Department continued, 'That your friend Mitchelberger is coming over at the end of June, just in time for the Waysgoose. The Vice-Chancellor has invited him.'

Predictably, this put the Snakenborg Professor into a tailspin. There are few events, if any, which senior Isleworth academics enjoy more than the annual printers' picnic. Traditionally for printers and a few important dignitaries only, this waysgoose had been expanded (some might say adulterated or debased) in recent decades to include departmental heads and a few other distinguished academics and even the little-loved University Visitor,[148] a man reviled for his meddling in matters which he was intellectually unequipped to comprehend, as well as the printers[149] and non-printing staff of

---

148 Officially called the Ἀλλοτριοεπίσκοπος, or Busybody.

149 Unlike several lesser British university presses which it would be churlish to name, Isleworth has not only retained its substantial printing division, it had increased it in recent years, absorbing a number of printing staff from Cambridge University Press, just

Isleworth University Press who had always participated. Invitation to the event was in the gift of the Vice-Chancellor in his role as head of the Syndics of Isleworth University Press, the grandly-titled Archetypographus. Under the present Vice-Chancellor, this event had inevitably become known as Teddy Behr's picnic. Gray had the finely die-stamped, chamfered and gilt-edged invitation on his mantlepiece (and a shoeboxful from previous years) and he did not relish the idea of this wonderful occasion being invaded by an uncouth American paltroon[150] who had done his best to undermine his career. On the other hand, he was rather looking forward to his confrontation with Mitchelberger who, he was sure, would make a fool of himself about the Madonna. At this point, Gray became so obsessed with this scenario that he forgot to ask Merlin what he knew about the first murder victim, which was unfortunate as he was then shooed out by an officious nurse who told him that he was tiring the patient.

On leaving the hospital, relieved to find Merlin in reasonable health but distressed that he had failed to ask him any pertinent questions, Gray wandered aimlessly through the Shallows, passing the cottage where Alfred Tebbit (or Tebbut), Molecatcher-in-Ordinary to George III, had lived quietly until he was hanged for treason in 1777. There was a subject for a book, he felt, something more worthy of his talents than *A Brief History of the Letter K* on which he had squandered so much effort, not to mention these absurd murders and the unmysterious 'mystery' of the Isleworth Madonna. Although they concerned him intimately, they did not appeal to him intellectually. He turned his mind instead to the vexatious issue of finding a suitable bottle of whisky to take Merlin on his next visit to the hospital. A less discerning drinker might have been fobbed off with a bog-standard Islay single malt at forty quid a bottle, but Merlin was a connoisseur in this as in so many other

---

as they had done with staff from Oxford University Press and Alden Press years before.
150   Not to be confused by the Dutch-American word *patroon*, although there may be, for all I know, some overlap.

matters. Well, at least he was in the right place to find something, right in the heart of the medical (i.e. heavy-drinking) area of the campus. He seemed to remember that there was a little off-licence around here somewhere which specialised in rare Scotch whiskies (and even a few English Welsh, Irish, Japanese and North American distillations, too). This looked like the very cobbled street, winding away from the hospital car park (that made sense – no busy consultant would want to journey too far for a wee dram). First he came across a bagel shop. What on earth possessed anyone to eat these dreary objects? Once, convinced that there must be some hidden virtue in them, Professor Gray had made his own but they had been identical to the tasteless commercial variety and he had never eaten one since, even on the one occasion that he had been rather forcefully encouraged to do so by the Chief Rabbi.[151] Equally out of place, to Gray's mind, was the next shop, a haberdasher's. Then there was a fine, old-fashioned butcher's shop, its windows garlanded with plump pork sausages. Across the road, he saw, and ignored, a bank, a dry cleaner and an estate agent. Essential though their services were, they held no charm, no beauty, no allure. Next came a handsome, old-fashioned greengrocer's shop, not bearing the Snakenborg name but displaying large cauliflowers, gay orange carrots (and a few bunches of Afghan purple), celeriac, kohlrabi, pink fir apple potatoes and salad vegetables in neat rows. Then there was an establishment bearing the word '𝕬𝖓𝖙𝖎𝖖𝖚𝖊𝖘' in an ill-wrought blackletter, although '𝕵𝖚𝖓𝖐' would have been a more accurate description of the articles displayed in the window. When he reached the sex shop, he was beginning to think that he either had the wrong street or that the off-licence had closed down, but there it was on the other side of the street, sandwiched between the Green Man public house and the offices of Isleworth Biotechnology plc, one of the University's commercial spin-offs.

---

151 An entirely different occasion to the one in which he was forced to drink Château Lafite-Rothschild at gunpoint. I'm afraid there is no space to go into *that* story here and I am not entirely satisfied that Professor Gray's memory of the incident is entirely accurate. He was, after all, under considerable stress at the time.

It was an unassuming and rather dirty shop and little could be discerned behind the grimy window except a few bottles of Barolo and one of akvavit. The words 'Douglas Bros. Fine Wines & Spirits' displayed in chipped yellow paint against a dark green background above the window were bluntly contradicted by the notice above the door which named a K. Patel as the licensee. The Snakenborg Professor entered in a mood of quiet pessimism engendered by the outward appearance of the shop. Inside, however, all was neat and clean and the bell triggered by the opening door summoned a smartly-dressed young man of Indian appearance.

'Why, Professor Gray!' he exclaimed, 'I didn't know you ever made it down here.'

'Occasionally. Do you have time to work here and complete your PhD, Ketan? The last time we met, your thesis was running six months late.'

'Well, you know, Prof., I've had to order up a lot of material from Babeş-Bolyai University and I'm still waiting for some of it.'

'You'll forgive me for saying that "Weaving History and Mythology in Ottoman Transylvania" is a very challenging subject and one I'm not really qualified to supervise. And the title is ambiguous.'

'Deliberately, of course. Anyway, Prof., what can I do for you?'

'I'm looking for an unusual single malt to cheer up Professor Le-Maistre. He's in hospital.'

'Sorry to hear that. One of the good guys, eh? Thought I hadn't seen him on the squash courts recently. What sort of whisky does he like?'

'Oh, pretty catholic tastes, I think. Highland, Lowland, Speyside, Islay, but it has to be *very* good.'

'Well, I have a very interesting, if pricey, Lowland. Nineteen-year-old Saint Magdalene bottled in 1998. They turned the distillery into housing, can you believe? Rich, complex and subtle. A snip at ninety quid.'

Gray handed over his credit card and gazed around him. There was a strange mixture of single malts, fine sherries, Scandinavian and east European firewaters and cheap (but, according to Ketan, excellent) Bulgarian red wine.

'Don't let him drink it neat,' said the young man, handing over the bottle and returning Gray's card; 'It's cask strength, 63.8%.'

Gray acknowledge this and left with his precious amber cargo in an elegantly-printed paper bag. As he exited the off-licence, he glimpsed a familiar figure exiting the greengrocer's shop. Millicent Behr was dressed in a summery cotton dress – white with a few discreet elements of colour – which swung seductively as she moved. He considered retiring to the safety of the off-licence but hesitated a second too long and she turned to see him.

'Hello, Professor Gray,' she said and, although she gave a bright smile, he felt there was a coolness in her manner. It might not have been unrelated to his having deserted her for the delights of Twickenham Studios the other night. It should have been a merciful relief after her previous vampishness but somehow it made him just as uneasy. He replied stiffly and bent down to retie a shoelace – one of the constant irritations in his life; when he unbent he was both relieved and a little puzzled to see that she had disappeared.

Gray wandered back, owling around Em Quad before ascending to his rooms. It occurred to him, possibly for the first time, that quadrangles, by their very angularity (which forced one to turn ninety degrees suddenly four times in each complete circuit), were less suited to deep contemplation than circular or oval enclosures. Despite that, he was convinced that a circular or elliptical colonnade would be entirely unsatisfactory, and very vulgar, except where it was on the exterior surface a structure – and even then he found the idea repugnant. Exhausted by too much thinking, he collapsed once more into his leather armchair and, almost immediately, fell asleep. Without Pugwash to wake him, it was possible he would sleep for hours. Some small part of his brain remained active and imagined that the dust around him, deprived of the daytime warmth which helped keep it in suspension, would slowly descend upon the carpets, the books, his desk and himself.

21: A Threatening Letter

I HAVE ALLUDED BEFORE briefly to the Isleworth microclimate. Like Isleworthians themselves, it is of a rather insular disposition. It is somewhat damp and a little chilly in winter, though seldom really sodden or bitterly cold. The springs are usually crisp and bright and occasionally very warm. The summers are often hot, though seldom *very* hot. The autumns are sometimes warm and sometimes cool. In brief, the climate, like the inhabitants, is generally of a temperate nature, not given to extremes of any kind, but a little unpredictable.

If Professor Gray was tired that evening, it was not heat exhaustion which brought it on but mental exertion, or possibly a bug. In any case, he did not sleep for long. It was perhaps those few synapses which had been engaged in the poetical contemplation of dust in his rooms which alerted him to the approaching dusk and advised him to go home and feed Pugwash. Or perhaps it was some quite different part of his brain, the amygdala, one supposes, which shook him awake (quite gently, I imagine) at 7.45 or there-abouts. It is also possible that it was not concern for his furry friend but the creak of steps on the ancient stairs and a sense of danger which awoke him. We shall never know, since Professor Gray himself is unclear on the matter.

Then, fully alert, he heard the distinctive wobble-creak-wobble of a plank, an old and blackened timber removed from the foredeck of the warship Peter Pomegranate during minor repairs made in 1547 after the Battle of Pinkie Cleugh.[152] It had been an ill-hewn and creaky plank and still a little green when the ship was constructed

---

152 This plank postdates the staircase as a whole by nearly 150 years and was part of a widening programme necessitated by the extraordinary weight and girth of Sir Peter Lambert, Her Majesty's Remembrancer and University Busybody in the 1560s. It is said that the weight of the life-size statue of him erected in the great hall at Uxbridge Court was responsible for the building's collapse in 1647, although a minor earth tremor could equally have been to blame.

at Pompey in 1510 and, though now blackened with age and dirt, was creaky still. The unmistakable wobble-creak-wobble told Gray that someone was directly outside his rooms, not an unusual circumstance, even in the early evening. Nonetheless, he felt a sense of dread which retarded his response and, almost immediately, he heard other distinctive creaks, more of a creak-creak-wobble-creak, as the unknown visitor descended the oaken flight.

Gray, his fear receding with every creaking step, slowly unrumpled himself and gently levered his corporeal being out of the comfort of the armchair. He noticed in passing that there had been no undue precipitation of dust upon his person or his possessions during his brief dialogue with Morpheus. Such is the power of the unconscious mind that it was some thirty seconds before he was perfectly convinced of this.

Eventually, and with a certain circumspection, he crept towards the door and opened it noiselessly (as he kept it well oiled with 3-in-One borrowed from his bicycle toolkit). There was no lingering figure in the evening gloom, he could be sure, as the stair well was reasonably well illuminated by a series of fifteenth-century diamond-paned windows. There was no sound of breathing, nor a single creak, except in each case those belonging to the Snakenborg Professor himself. There was, however, on the landing, upon the aforementioned wobble-creak-wobble plank, a white envelope, the C5 size intended to hold sheets of A4 paper folded only once. As Gray bent down to pick it up, he could see no writing on it – something out-of-the-ordinary, surely? It was probably some completely harmless note from an undergraduate explaining why an essay was late, although the envelope was pristine and undergraduates these days seemed to have a fatal attraction to dirt and grime as, indeed, they had in his youth, though then they had the added excuse of fountain pens and even dip pens (although he was far too young to be a slave to dip-pens, he had been known to scratch out his lecture notes with them). In any case, few of the modern breed would use an envelope, or even paper. Most essays and excuses were conveyed to him by the soulless agency of electronic mail or SMS.

He returned to his study holding the envelope by a corner to avoid obliterating prints and turned on the light over his large oak desk, searching the right desk drawer for a pack of surgical gloves he thought he'd left in there after a previous investigation; they were not there so he scavenged the Marigolds from the kitchen. Wearing these clumsy, jaundiced monstrosities, and not feeling at all like the valiant forensic scientists of televisual legend, he sliced open the envelope with a paper knife as sharp as a surgeon's scalpel, the present of a passing Emir from a gulf state who had once requested (and received) Gray's help in a matter of some delicacy. My lips are sealed, as was the envelope.

Inside was a single sheet of thin, white paper. Before he unfolded it, Gray noted that it was puckered and discoloured; perhaps it was from a student after all, a notion soon dispelled when he opened it. The age-old manner of sending anonymous communications composed of letters clipped from local newspapers was not, it seemed, dead, no doubt providing a welcome adjunct to the circulation figures. Local because Gray, whose typographical understanding did not begin or end with the crook-backed fs so notoriously associated with Thomas J. Wise,[153] thought he recognised certain distinctive features of the *Richmond and Twickenham Times*. The letters were very neatly cut out but had been arranged in that jauntily haphazard fashion prized by the composers of such missives. The general effect, Gray had to admit, was rather pleasing, if contrived. The message was simple, though somewhat lacking in precision[154] (that, at least, would be typical of his students): 'Stop interfering or your friend dies.' Interfering in what? Which friend? These were the first questions which sprang to his mind, before another sur-

---

153   It is interesting to note, however, that these fs which played such a prominent part in the evidence of his forgeries were actually no proof at all.
154   Those who have worked with Gray or studied under him know how much he detests imprecision, especially in the written word. I can only imagine the horror with which he would have read such a letter.

faced – why go to the trouble of cutting up letters when one could simply print the message out on one of the many communal laser and inkjet printers around the university? Far simpler and at least as difficult to trace. For effect, perhaps, or because it was the work of an unhinged mind. But all this speculation would have to wait. He must return to Richmond where Pugwash would be pining, not for his owner but for his supper. A cat's life, as Gray had reflected more than once before, was very simple compared with that of a Professor of Cultural History, especially one who had just received a threatening letter. For safe keeping, he popped it into the ancient ballot box by his desk which, in a previous existence, had helped to re-elect a bevy (if that is the correct collective noun) of dull MPs to a certain rotten borough.

22: Another Threatening Letter

PROFESSOR GRAY DISMOUNTED from his Brompton, un-
screwed the fastenings, folded it in a matter of a few seconds and placed it in its carrying sack before unlocking the
door to his very humble terrace house on Albert Road, Richmond;
he proceeded to take both it and himself inside. He locked the
door, picked up the post and was just in time to see Pugwash march
down the stairs and make a quick exit through the catflap to the
small patio garden. It was typical of his furry friend that he would
sleep all day and only rouse himself when Gray returned.

He flung the mail unexamined on the dining table and went into
the kitchen to put out some vile-smelling food for Pugwash and
fixing himself two thumbs of Black Bush and a dash of over-chlo-
rinated tap-water (sacrilege, no doubt, but he was no purist, and
when he thought of how many people had drunk this same water
already, he was quite pleased to have a little chlorine).

Returning to his sitting/dining room, he collapsed into the sad
old sofa, his companion of many years, its springs and stuffing sag-
ging under the melancholy effects of old age, its once-bright cloth
now frayed and faded, like its owner a little tired and uncared for.

Despite his earlier rest, he felt tired until the first gulp of whisky hit the back of his throat and he felt, in a contradictory way,
both more relaxed and more alert. He put his iPod into the Bose
docking station and played Boyce's *Solomon*; a nagging ache in his
temples slowly dissipated. He could feel his toes unclench, a sure
sign that he was fully relaxed. He glanced around the room at all
the familiar objects – the tatty furniture, moderately good paintings, obscure mantelpiece ornaments, including a First World War
Mills bomb (without the explosive) and a small and remarkably
ugly twelfth-century figurine, purportedly depicting Joseph of Ari-
mathea with his thorny staff. It had a greengage-hued glaze and was
a rare pilgrim piece of a sort sold to visitors of Glastonbury Abbey

in the days of Henry of Blois; then as now ecclesiastical gift shops did a roaring trade. Then his eyes flitted to the letters on the dining table. Was there a plain white envelope like the one he received earlier? He decided he was becoming paranoid and, rather than bother with the post, he flicked on the television. Tiring rapidly of the BBC television news which, as ever now, ignored wars, famine, earthquakes and riots in favour of sport and 'celebrities' he'd never heard of, he turned the set off again and went over to look at the post. Even a threatening letter would come as welcome relief from televisual bilge.

There was the usual unappealing mixture of Reader's Digest competitions, bills and 'confidential' letters about get-rich-quick schemes. How, he wondered, had he ended up on someone's sucker list? There was also a plain white envelope of C5 size, but this one bore a laser-printed label and had come through the post. Nonetheless, the paper and construction of the envelope looked identical to the anonymous warning. He had no gloves of any description at home, other than some cumbersome gardening gloves, so he threw caution to the wind and handled it with his bare hands. It seemed to be empty until he tipped it upside-down. A thin sheet of A4 paper fell onto the carpet. He picked it up. It was not a letter but just a photograph printed out from a computer, a photograph, clearly taken covertly, of himself and Arundhati at the Garden of Earthly Delights. One could just see a massive shoulder, undoubtedly belonging to the Emeritus Professor of Chemistry, beside the librarian. Gray thought he recognised Arundhati's dress as the one she'd been wearing the other day when they'd been discussing the Madonna. Someone had crossed out her face crudely in red felt-tip. So, it was the lovely librarian who was being threatened, and presumably it was the Madonna which he was required to cease investigating. He felt suddenly depressed. He'd assumed that the friend referred to in the previous note had been Merlin, who could look after himself, or Chummy Beetleson who was never around these days. But Arundhati! He could not put her at risk; he'd have to stop the investigation immediately.

He poured himself another Black Bush and sat very quietly, sipping it slowly, thinking of going to bed. Pugwash was already asleep in his basket by the radiator.

Still on the sofa, he started to drop off, thinking of Arundhati, Merlin and Chummy. He wondered where Chummy was.

23: The Manifold Charms of Heathrow

AS IT HAPPENS, Reginald Thurgood Beetleson, commonly known as Chummy, was some thirty-six thousand feet above the earth's surface at that moment in a mercilessly uncomfortable Club World class window seat (he always insisted on a window seat – he wanted to know if an engine fell off) of the British Airways 22.55 flight from Singapore due into Heathrow at 5 in the bloody morning. He pitied the poor buggers under the flight-path (of whom one was a gently-sleeping Professor Gray, still not a-bed).

Beetleson wondered where he could get a decent breakfast when he landed. Certainly not at Heathrow and he could think of nowhere between Heathrow and the University which could be relied upon to rustle up a full English. Indeed, to call the barren corridor between Heathrow and Isleworth a gastronomic desert would be an unwarranted attack on the culinary delights of deserts. Even the most resourceful Kalahari bushman would been alarmed at the lack of digestible food in the Heathrow hinterland. As for the campus itself, there was at least one oasis, Merlin's house in Boswell Terrace, but he'd heard that Merlin was in prison. Pity. For the moment he'd have to content himself with sucking on sugar-free mints. And he mustn't have too many of them. They contained sorbitol (hadn't they heard of aspartame?) and could give him a gippy tummy. Their charm was beginning to pall in any case. Perhaps another glass or two of wine? He'd like to stretch his legs (and avoid DVT) but the fat woman in the aisle seat was asleep and it was just too much effort to get past her. Just as well he didn't want to go to the loo.

Perhaps, he thought, he'd get the Heathrow Express, a mere nineteen minutes into Paddington, and have breakfast there. He imagined plump pork sausages, black pudding, bacon, fried eggs, fried bread, fried tomatoes and a plenitude of vast field mushrooms. Beetlesons have thrived on saturated fat since the dawn of time. A large pot of coffee and some orange juice. Or some tea, as long as it was PG Tips, not some flavourless crap. Beetleson knew what he liked and he was damned well going to get it. It seemed absurd to divert away from Isleworth and then have to double back, but what was the alternative? He could call in on Gerrish Gray (whom he had to see in any case). Gray was something of a gourmand but Beetleson suspected he was too lazy to spend much time cooking. He imagined opening his fridge to find nothing but a head of lettuce and a few tomatoes. And a larder full of porridge oats. No, there was no point visiting Gray for breakfast, although he had urgent business with him. He wondered if the Garden of Earthly Delights opened in time for breakfast. He doubted it, but if they did they would undoubtedly provide a superlative spread. He thought of their wonderful steak and kidney puddings, the gravy rich and flavoursome. Such thoughts made him very peckish and he sucked on another sugar-free mint – sorbitol be damned.

Before he could get anywhere near a breakfast table, though, he had to get through customs and that might be a little tricky. Prosperous, middle-aged, trim and rubicund and wearing an immaculate pin-stripe suit, Beetleson was just the sort whom the UK Border Agency suspected of illegal activities. After all, who wears a suit these days, especially when travelling? It had been Beetleson's misfortune to have been brought up to believe that dressing well was an inviolable social obligation. Indeed, he still felt a pang of conscience that he didn't wear a dinner jacket for supper at home. No doubt his father had felt guilty for wearing a dinner jacket rather than evening dress. Perhaps it could all be traced back to an ancestor who had been a snappy dresser in the mead halls of the Anglo-Saxons. Or some ruff-necked courtier who'd thrown his cape onto a puddle for the Virgin Queen. The irony was that Beetleson had absolutely no interest in clothes. He could unerringly identify a bolt of the finest English cloth and the finest Savile Row tailoring, and that was what he had to wear, but it gave him no pleasure; it was an obligation.

If Beetleson hadn't been sartorially suspicious to the men in blue, the scent of Dutch gin which enveloped him might have attracted their attention. G&T, after all, was a spiv's drink, but at least spivs were discerning enough to drink London Dry and not the vulgar and effete Netherlandish distillation.[155] The customs officers were not to know that they were smelling the subtle botanicals of an aftershave only available from a little-known and somewhat exclusive hairdresser on the fringes of Mayfair, an establishment mercifully free from the raucous inanity of so-called celebrities; no doubt employing an exclusive hairdresser, especially one devoid of celebrities, would only have deepened their suspicions, had they known. Her Britannic Majesty's subject, Reginald Thurgood Beetleson, born Frome, Somerset, on 23 December 1948, seemed a little too perfect – a little too well-spoken, well-groomed, well-fed, well-dressed and well-heeled – and every petty official at every port of entry seemed to sense it. It did not help that he had things to hide. Not that there was anything illegal – no Beetleson in recorded history had ever been convicted of a criminal offence, nor even jay walking, nor littering – but, as so often, he was carrying things of a confidential nature, things that were better shielded from the bovine gaze of officialdom. He turned his attention back to a day-old copy of *Le Monde.* He only usually read it on Fridays for the book section but what the hell? Its very dullness (though not as marked as that of most of the newspapers available in Singapore) made a pleasant change from the vulgarity of *The Times,* the smugness of the *Guardian* and the low-brow nature of everything part of the *Daily Telegraph* other than the book reviews and business section.

---

155   Shockingly, London Dry gin is not required to be distilled in London, or even the United Kingdom.

24: Dying is Easy

'Dying is easy; comedy is hard.'[156]

G RAY HAD SLEPT badly on the sofa, partly from worry and partly through discomfort, not helped by Pugwash who scratched his arm playfully whenever the professor looked like falling into a deeper sleep. Eventually he dragged himself to the bathroom where he brushed his teeth and then to his bedroom. He climbed into bed and, whether due to fatigue or Pugwash's temporary absence, fell into a deep though troubled sleep from which he did not awake until Pugwash roused him punctually at six. A foodless cat, as even the most unworldly academic knows, is not a force of nature to be trifled with.

It was immediately clear to him that he must tell Clanarsh about the notes and, regrettably, he would also have to inform the Proctor. He rather hoped that the Metropolitan Police would somehow manage to wrest control of the investigations into the Madonna and the Snakenborg Gallery murder from the Isleworth Bulls. It was far too early to contact either guardian of the law so he contented himself with eating an oily and satisfying *skeddan jiarg,* or Manx kipper. The look which Pugwash gave him left him in no doubt that he was suspected of eating the cat's perquisites but he bore the accusation lightly.

Should you have gained the erroneous impression that the life of a professor at Isleworth University is (apart from the odd murder) one of carefree idleness, I apologise. It is not, as far as I am aware, a requirement for a professor of poetry at any British university – and I confess there are lamentably few of us – to be a master of narrative prose style. It may be that in telling the story in the same plain and unadorned manner which I employ in everyday life, I

---

156   Edmund Kean.

have omitted much of the humdrum detail of academic drudgery at this august institution which did not seem germane to the story behind the strident headlines. It is clearly time to set the record straight and tell you frankly that, having finished his kipper, I have no doubt that Professor Gray spent an hour or two, either in correcting student essays or in some other academic duty appropriate to his station.

Having corrected essays, or whatever else it was that he did after breakfast, Gray slung upon his back the same leather satchel he had taken to prep school every day in his pre-teens; it was a little worn now, but still robust and far more appealing than those amorphous backpacks manufactured from synthetic fibres. The usual academic papers had been augmented by the second anonymous note. He carried his Brompton from the back garden to the front porch and unfolded it, locking the three nuts in place, all within ten seconds. He mounted it and was soon coasting down Albert Road, turning left on Sheen Road and forking left at the First Church of Christ, Scientist, past the former Register Office on Spring Terrace and the Dr Lee's surgery in Paradise Road, past the parish church of St Mary Magdalene (containing a memorial to the great actor, Edmund Kean), past a new building on the site of the old police station, Pizza Express and Waterstone's bookshop on Red Lion Street; the road had changed its name three times in about a hundred yards. He took a right in George Street and then a swift left to turn down the cobbled Water Lane (though cobbles are the enemy of cyclists), swerving right when the Slug and Lettuce appeared on his left and then hurtling past the White Cross public house in which he had occasionally been held an uncomplaining captive by the high tide, awash with Thames water and Young's Best (in the days when it was brewed in Wandsworth rather than Bedford). Now he was cycling beside the Thames, with the large lawn of Trumpeter's House on his right, past the Palladian villa known as Asgill House, past Palace Lane, for the remains of Henry VII's palace are just around here, and under the railway bridge, now thundering from a passing train, and under the concrete supports of the art deco road bridge. Cycling beside the Old Deer Park a little way, he came to Richmond Lock and there dismounted to carry his bicycle across the footbridge. On the other side, he remounted and cycled along the river, on the Isleworth side. He took a turning left which brought him onto the A3004 and soon to Old Isleworth. You know the way to the University from there, of course, the wide avenues and narrow winding lanes (although the route is somewhat more involved by car), so I shall not bore you with a detailed description. He did not go past Bosworth Terrace on this occasion but skirted the picturesque water meadow made famous by Turner's painting (now, sadly, said to be in a bank vault in Kuala Lumpur), dotted with small black Dexters rather than the large white Isleworth cattle the artist had depicted so beautifully in 1805.[157]

Soon, sooner than he would have liked, he arrived at the South-West Gate. Because it was still early, there was no porter on duty and the large gates were locked, obliging him to dismount, open the door-within-a-door, gnarled and wormed with age, by rotating its stiff iron ring, and to lift his Brompton through. Such are the trials of the modern academic at an ancient place[158] of learning.

His rooms had lost some of their comfortable and welcoming atmosphere since he had found the anonymous message on his door step. Where before he had admired the dust particles dancing in the sun, the air felt still and lifeless, the bookshelves looked drab. The Persian carpet which yesterday was a glimmering antique which at the mere uttering of secret incantation might conceivably have carried him swiftly to distant lands now looked pitifully threadbare, and certainly not airworthy. The only thing which had not changed was his grey, university-issue computer, the scuffed case and monitor looking as cheap and plasticky as ever (and almost old enough to feature in the *Plastiquarian* magazine), the brightness nob still

157   It is sometimes said that Turner could not draw *human* figures. However, his portrayal of Isleworth cattle, in all their mud-spattered glory, is unparalleled.

158   I might almost have said 'pace', for while the standard of scholarship is high, the tempo at Isleworth is *andante* rather than *presto*.

broken, the keyboard (which possessed a strange attraction to sweat and sebaceous secretions) grubby, the spaghetti of grey cables still an undisciplined mess.

He was getting paranoid now and looked around for signs that anyone might have entered in his absence. It seemed unlikely; there were two robust Banham locks on the door to his rooms – rather out of keeping with the ancient oak door but necessitated by the growth of crime, even on the Isleworth campus. He checked his desk. The first anonymous letter was there and his petty cash box, black enamelled mild steel of dubious quality with red and gold lines for decoration, still held a strange assortment of currencies – euros, Louis d'ors, groats, some cartwheel pennies, florins, half-crowns and farthings, a silver threepence and two or three Bank of England dollars from the Napoleonic wars. An assortment of buttons made up for the insufficiency of legal tender; as Gray's great-aunt Morwenna had often opined, a good button would always keep its value.

He could find no sign of disturbance. Indeed, the layer of dust on almost every surface seemed to vouchsafe the inviolacy of his personal possessions – there was a cleaner who came in once a week and it was pretty clear that she had not touched a single surface in the study, which was just as Gray would have it. He wondered if he was becoming a little obsessive about dust but, given its ubiquity, could he not be? Did Sir Thomas Browne say anything about dust in his *Pseudodoxia Epidemica*? He must look it up. There is little doubt that he would have referred to a copy on *Early English Books in Print* then and there had his thoughts not been interrupted by a knock on the door. Such, as I have remarked before, are the trials of a modern academic.

It was Wendell Tallboy, an American of course. Gray was surprised and, he confessed, disappointed that he wasn't Wendell Tallboy the third or at least junior, to finish the effect. There had been Tallboys on the *Mayflower*, it was said (without a shred of truth), and Gray had little doubt that there had been previous Wendells in the family; it was simply the sort of inanity one expected from Americans.[159]

Tallboy managed to be lank without actually being tall; he gangled from an unexceptional height of six feet but he stooped his head and twisted his limbs as though he could only just fit into Gray's study, a very lofty room by medieval standards. It was rather as though the foolish young man had swigged the contents of the bottle marked 'drink me' but had then failed to eat the cake marked 'eat me'. He was quiet and reticent, weighing every word carefully. He had the vocabulary and mien of a scholar but his command of written English, although technically good, was so corrupted by dullness that it was quite impossible to divine what he was trying to say, leaving Gray to wonder whether Tallboy was a clever young man who was unable to express his thoughts in writing or an idiot who managed to seem reasonably intelligent in conversation. The ability to produce the latter sort of person had been the most obvious (some would say only) achievement of the British educational system, wreaking lasting damage on the country's commercial and political elite. Gray had seen enough of the American elite to realise that the British were not alone in their ability to turn out glib morons.

'Wendell, what can I do for you?'

Tallboy shook his head slowly before uttering a word, 'Oh, hi, Prof. I was just passing and I found this outside your door.' He proffered an unaddressed C5 envelope, 'Oh, and by the way, can I have an extension on my slave trade essay? It's a lot of work, you know? Some of those sources you mentioned are rather difficult to track down.'

---

159   I am afraid that, despite his many fine qualities, Professor Gray's prejudices against Americans, art historians and many other sections of society are somewhat unfortunate, although I can hardly contest his assertion that an American is 'one who does not know his ass from his arse'. However, Wendell Tallboy has attended my classes on sprung rhythm and I judge him to be a complete idiot, if only because he sat through 'The Wreck of the *Deutschland*' without the hint of a yawn.

'OK, one week,' said Gray, shooing Tallboy out of the room; he was too disturbed by the sight of the envelope to put up a fight. As it turned out, it only contained a flyer for the SCR annual bunfight. Not at all sinister, but it was surprising that it was not addressed. He chucked it on his in-pile (there was a single pile, tall and precipitous, for 'in' and 'out').

It was now about nine and he decided he should phone Clanarsh. He pulled out the Chief Inspector's card and dialled the number. It went to voicemail and there was no mobile number on the card. Next, the decidedly unpleasant duty of phoning Vortimer Williams. The Proctor's phone also went to voicemail and, if Gray had once had his mobile number, he had forgotten it – thrown it in the bin, no doubt. It would be on the University's internal telephone list but he couldn't be bothered to look it up. In retrospect, it was probably fortunate that Williams had not answered his phone. He would no doubt insist that Gray hand over the letters while Gray felt that the Met's capacity to analyse them was probably far superior to the Bulls'. And he almost liked Clanarsh.

He switched on his computer which, being old, clunked, spluttered and whirred, booting up far more slowly than it should. It was still on XP and its Pentium processor would probably struggle with Windows 7 and fail to install Windows 8 or 10 at all, if the Computer Facilities Department ever deigned to supply it. Mind you, it struggled to run XP, too. Despite these limitations, there was an email waiting for him from Dr Habib of the University of Cairo on the apparently deliberate mistranslations from Egyptian into Greek in the Rosetta Stone. Something at the same time both fascinating and outside his (what he felt to be very narrow) area of competence. There was also a message from Chummy. Much though he liked the elusive Mr Beetleson, Gray seldom found he could understand him and the email did not prove too be an exception to the rule: 'In the Nile, crocodile. Sent from my iPhone.' His previous communication, sent from Changi Airport, read simply, 'Make mine a marmalade.' It had a ring to it.

He scanned in both threatening letters, handling them carefully to avoid further contamination, and sent the images to Clanarsh's email (a.clanarsh@met.police.uk should you be in need of a first-class detective) with a covering message. He'd hold off sending them to Vortimer Williams for the moment, perhaps forever.

He turned his attention to the (only slightly) more welcome matter of Lionel Pendover's essay, purporting to be a statistical analysis of English East India Company commercial activity from 1757 to 1857. This was no doubt a worthy area of study but Gray knew almost as much about statistics as he did about Flemish weavers, medieval horseshoes and the history of Barnwell Priory, while Pendover's grasp of the subject was obviously lacking. Would there be any point in sending him for remedial statistics? Most historians managed quite well without a thorough understanding of statistical method, though many would benefit immeasurably from a better grounding in it. The trouble was that he suspected that Pendover was fundamentally stupid. Why else would the young man choose to write on a subject of which he understood so little? He stumbled not only over the statistics but also over the Persian used as a *lingua franca* by John Company. Gray knew no Persian but he'd never attempted an area of study which required it.

'3/100. This is hopeless. You are stupid, innumerate and semiliterate,' he scrawled in the top lefthand corner of the first page. Fortunately for Gray, Isleworth had (and continues to have) a more enlightened attitude to rigorous academic criticism than the University of Nottingham.[160] Indeed, it was generally agreed within Isleworth that the quality of the undergraduate intake in recent years was uninspiring. If that were true of Isleworth, the mind boggled to think what Nottingham undergraduates were like.[161]

---

160   A Nottingham lecturer, Tony Fisher, was recently (2014) criticised by the School of English for describing his students on Facebook as idiots and semiliterate. Although Gray considered the right to criticise students to be sacrosanct, his dislike of Facebook put him squarely in the undergraduates' camp.
161   Gray, like many Isleworth academics of his generation, shows an unreasonable contempt for newer universities, including Oxford and Cambridge.

25: The Prophesies of Merlin

Merlin, by delivering these and many other prophecies, caused in all who were present an admiration at the ambiguity of his expressions.[162]

ANOTHER DAY, ANOTHER (Bank of England) dollar. Gray rolled (was he getting fat?) out of bed, narrowly missing a Pugwash *couchant* wrapped around a pair of the Professor's second-best stout brown walking shoes (size 10½ extra wide). He tramped barefooted to the bathroom, shaved with an ancient Gillette, brushed his teeth with a particularly minty brand of toothpaste and launched himself sideways, rather in the manner of a type 45 destroyer ready for fitting-out, into the bath, rather than the Clyde. He noted that the displacement was substantial and the water mercifully free from the fearful unguents (a.k.a. giant slime mould) which used to contaminate his bath with bubbles and scents when his ex-wife had been around. If he missed this or any other aspect of their marriage, he never admitted it. The bath he took today was free from any suds other than those from an undistinguished-looking bar of soap, the product of Merlin's laboratory, smelling of marigolds and something else (Gray was not sure what, only that it was not unpleasant); it did the job as most soaps do. He lay back, absorbing the somewhat musky odour of the soap, and thought long and deeply (as he was wont to do). He was not entirely convinced by Merlin's story of the nutmeg poisoning. According to an ancient book on poisons (bought by Gray many years ago from a book barrow in Milbank), myristicin, the active ingredient, was a monoamine oxidase inhibitor (whatever that means) and could, at least in theory, cause problems for some people when consumed with cheese; but if it were *that* dangerous, Merlin's cola would have wreaked havoc long ago, cheese-eating being very much

---

162 Geoffrey of Monmouth, *History of the Kings of Britain,* Book Viii, Chapter I.

a part of Isleworth culture.[163] Accidental nutmeg poisoning did not seem to explain the gallery death or provide Merlin with a get-out-of-jail-free card.

The completion of his cogitation and ablution coinciding, he rose out of the water like Poseidon or Apām Napāt, a god in his own bathroom as, indeed, all Englishmen are entitled to perceive themselves to be. If the thinking processes had been less than successful, the washing had achieved the desired effect and he rubbed himself briskly with a well-fluffed towel of Egyptian cotton.[164] Yes, his body did seem a little rounder than before, and not just at the waist. Glancing in the mirror, his once-craggy jaw[165] seemed less craggy than before, his eyes puffier. As for the rest... mercifully it was only a shaving mirror and the rest was hidden from view.[166] Thus refreshed and at least moderately dry, he strode back to his bedroom and flung on a set of suitably donnish clothes.[167] Having fed Pugwash, he was soon tucking into a hearty breakfast in which Bury black pudding played a not unimportant role. Fried eggs (from Cotswold Legbars) were there also, as was some toasted sourdough rye and the blackest Monsooned Malabar in a brightly ornamented mug worthy in its dimensions of Pantagruel himself. Pugwash played politely with a discarded morsel of bloater (it does

---

163   Whether that means we are what, I believe, are called 'surrender monkeys', I do not feel qualified to say.

164   The same raw material formerly employed to create the substrate for the old white five pound notes. If you wished to forge such notes today, you might do worse than start with superior bath towels of Egyptian cotton.

165   This is self-delusion on Professor Gray's part. His jaw was always almost effeminate in its lack of cragginess.

166   Which is, I'm sure, as the reader would wish it to be.

167   You will appreciate that it is remarkable enough that I should know his bathing habits and thought processes. I cannot be expected to know precisely what Professor Gray was wearing on this particularly day. It is reasonable to assume that he would have worn stout brown shoes, corduroy trousers, a plain cotton shirt with double cuffs and a tweed or perhaps lighter weight wool jacket. A tie, bearing or not bearing the crest of one of his universities or learned societies, is a distinct possibility. He usually wore grey lambswool socks, although other colours and yarns were not unheard of.

not do to eat Manx kippers every day and bloaters are, at least to some, an acceptable substitute).[168]

After breakfast he donned his bicycle clips (today a candy-striped pair enamelled by the University's artist in residence, Nancy Campbell) and headed for the door, satchel slung over one shoulder.

Again he followed the river towards Isleworth, this time veering left at the former university hospital, a gothic monstrosity brimming with turrets, designed by that indefatigable Victorian architect of fanciful water-towers, J. Flaxman Quayles.[169] A few further twists and turns took him to its gleaming white replacement, which would in a few years' time rival its predecessor for ugliness and would still be costing the tax-payer money under a PFI scheme long after it was obsolete. He folded his Brompton and locked it to a cycle stand before marching vigorously into the main vestibule and running up the stairs to the third floor.

When *Punch* lampooned Aubrey Beardsley as Aubrey Whiskersley, the magazine included a fair imitation of the artist's work depicting him lost in a sea of bed linen, and Gray was reminded of this image when he saw his friend again, though the hospital-issue pillows had none of the soft, comforting plumpness of those in the picture. In the precise line-drawings of Beardsley, Merlin would have taken on the simple whiteness of the paper but in real life his face was grey. His skin was slack and glistening, his face expressionless. Was this mere nutmeg poisoning? Gray was afraid that, rather than self-inflicted, Merlin's illness was the work of the anonymous letter-writer – 'Stop interfering or your friend dies.' Was his meddling responsible for his friend's ill health? Had he been responsible for Yllingstone's death? Who else might get hurt? His thoughts strayed to Arundhati. Was she safe? Was Chummy? Pugwash? It

168 Like other self-denying ordinances, Gray's periodic abstinence from Manx kippers cannot be considered an unalloyed success.
169 A man much lauded by the Royal Institute of British Architects for a body of work which made even the designs of Augustus Pugin seem subtle and understated by comparison. It is generally agreed outside the profession that Pugin and Quayles were responsible for more damage to Britain's built environment than the Luftwaffe. Some have levelled similar charges against the RIBA itself.

was a consolation to realise what a small circle of friends he had. It was rather the Isleworth way, the lecturers being reserved even with their students and colleagues. Some traced this attitude right back to the bitter feud between the University and William of Wykeham. It was perhaps not a coincidence that the University, having some ill-defined association with John of Gaunt, adopted its motto, *Tene Linguam,* (hold thy tongue) in the late fourteenth century.

'How are you, Merlin?'

The ashen-faced academic groaned slightly but forced a smile: 'It must have been something I ate.'

'You look tired. I wont stay but I'll pop in later. Is there anything I can get you?'

'I can't think why,' said Merlin, 'But I really feel like some gooseberries but it's too early in the year. Get me some Black Isleworth strawberries – and you should have some yourself. They are very good for you.'

Gray was surprised by the request but he smiled and confirmed that he would fetch some of the famous Isleworth fruit. He waved farewell and retreated to the corridor. Merlin really didn't look well.

He searched around and found a nurse, quite young and pretty in a well-scrubbed way,[170] and asked her who Merlin's doctor was. She told him that it was Dr Marleswain but that he would not be around until later. This, at least, was a piece of luck. 'Mad' Michael Marleswain was a good doctor and an old acquaintance whom Gray had first met during his investigation into Orcadian yellow cake found on a ship bound for Iran.

Gray felt he should stay but acknowledged to himself that there was nothing else he could do. He wandered slowly to the exit, saddled up and pedalled with all celerity to his rooms in Em Quad.

---

170 Prettiness can be scrubbed away altogether if one is not careful, although this was even more true in the days of carbolic soap.

26: The World of Glass

When a bullet strikes against a fixed obstacle, the particles of the latter are more or less displaced in offering resistance to its momentum; and this displacement is greater or less in proportion as the cohesive force of the body struck is less or more able to offer resistance to it.[171]

ALL WAS DULL and quiet in Gray's study and a gentle, unseasonal rain was falling outside. There were no threatening letters or messages on his voicemail. Even the dust seemed motionless. He switched on his computer which made its customary clunks and whirrs associated with booting up but the annoying jingles of the operating system had long been silenced, at his request, by a student with a talent for matters digital. As he had expected, there was an email announcing that Professor Mitchelberger would be arriving at the University on Thursday afternoon and would be inspecting the Madonna. Gray contemplated the forthcoming event with quiet satisfaction. However, he quickly reminded himself that the murders had yet to be solved and that his friend had been threatened – but which friend? Presumably Arunhati, but were there others? And how could he protect them?

Gray felt powerless. He couldn't even resort, as he so often did when inspiration failed, to watching the hypnotic motion of dust particles. They seemed to be entirely absent this morning. He knew they must be there but some condition of the light prevented him from observing their erratic descent. He thought again that Sir Thomas Browne, when not writing on *Urn Burials,* must have written copiously on dust. Like John Aubrey and Gray himself, the man had been something of a wool-gatherer, a quality which Gray much admired and felt was essential in the academic mind, although not all his colleagues were in accord. Even Gray admit-

---

171 John Boucher, *A Treatise on Rifle Projectiles,* London: Charles and Edwin Leyton, 1856, p. 50.

ted that paid leisure, which was how he rightly described his own vocation, held dangers, if not in wool-gathering *per se,* then in a more pervasive woolliness of thought and sclerosis of the brain. This held no danger to Gray himself, who was anything but lazy, and his occasional lapses into casual thought processes were used to re-assess his assumptions and recalibrate his brain; indeed, a few minutes contemplating the apparent absence of dust in the air had as satisfactorily revitalised his intellectual resources as observing the particles themselves might reasonably have been expected to. Within a quarter of an hour, his reasoning was as sharp as it had ever been and, if he still did not know the identity of the murderer or murderers, he felt sure that he was getting closer.

There was a knock at the door, a sharp, precision knock: rap-dah-dap; and, more remarkably, it had not been prefixed by a wobble-creak-wobble. Someone very light on his toes; Gray imagined a furtive sneak-thief or an anorexic girl and was rather surprised to open the door to the robust and betweeded form of Detective Chief Inspector Clanarsh. Even at this hour, there was an urgency about the policeman's manner quite out of keeping with the air of quiet contemplation in Gray's study. His arrival threatened to disturb the tranquil rock-pool that was Gray's mind. The Snakenborg Professor was, if you care for metaphors, the vestal virgin who kept the fire of introspection safe from guttering in the damp and blustery Isleworth zephyrs.

'I came as soon as I saw your email,' said Clanarsh striding purposefully into the room without waiting for an invitation. 'Just got back from a case in Harrogate. You wouldn't have some coffee, would you? The stuff at the Yard is undrinkable.'

Gray, who always welcomed the opportunity to brew a pot of Monsooned Malabar, tipped some of the dark, glistening beans into the grinder while he boiled a kettle of water, bringing the two together in a coffee pot of strange and antique construction and apparently a product of the Sèvres factory.[172]

---

172   Said to have belonged to Alexandre Dumas père and the only thing which ensured

There are too many words, don't you think...' Clanarsh began, 'Too many words in the English language.'

'One can never have too many words,' replied the Don, a man of well-established verbosity.

'One can certainly have too many words in a book or a speech or a poem, many would be better half as long.'

'That may be true,' Gray replied without conviction, 'But a large repertoir of words is an advantage.'

'Perhaps, Professor, although many writers – Samuel Beckett, for instance – might disapprove. Anyway, it got me thinking about your notes. They are plain, simple, direct...'

'But they are far from unambiguous. They are imprecise.'

'Exactly! The writer is either unable to express his- or herself or is deliberately avoiding doing so.'

'I can't see why he or she should be deliberately ambiguous, and I think the melodramatic use of cut-out letters – a time-consuming technique which potentially provides additional clues to the culprit's identity – points to a disordered mind. Someone whose emotions over-rule the rational mind. A nut-job, as we academics say.'

'I'm afraid you're right, Professor...'

'Gerrish, please.'

'... Er, Gerrish, and call me Al, although the term "nut-job" is frowned upon by the Metropolitan Police. But whether the letter-writer is responsible for the murders is another matter. You'd be surprised how many crazies come out of the woodwork when a case hits the headlines.'

'My main concern at the moment is the threat to my friend or friends. I have no idea whose life is threatened, other than Dr Datt. It's very oddly unspecific.'

---

the completion of *Le Comte de Monte-Cristo*. No doubt such a pot, dating from the late eighteenth century, heavily gilded and sporting a pastoral scene after the manner of Claude, would have been much prized by collectors, had not the gilding been heavily rubbed and the spout broken and riveted at least twice. In perfect condition it would have been far too showy for the Professor's taste, and far too valuable for his purse.

'And, unfortunately, with a clear threat to a single individual, there'd be just about a snowball's chance in hell that the Met's budget could stretch to some sort of protection for a few days, but a threat, probably from a harmless nutter, to anyone who might be considered a friend of yours leaves us unable to do anything – except to catch the culprit or culprits as soon as possible. And, of course, warn everyone. You'd better draw up a complete list of your friends and give it to me. But I'll leave it to you to warn them.'

'It will be a mercifully short list,' said Gray grimly; 'I'm most worried about the Librarian, Dr Datt, although she's not as defenceless as she looks – she has a black belt in kick-boxing, or something of the sort.'

'Of limited use when you're in the sights of a sniper rifle like the one which killed Yllingsone,' said Clanarsh.

'I felt the bullet pass me,' said Gray; 'I wondered if it might have been meant for me rather than him.'

'Anything's possible, but Yllingstone's connection with the Tweezle brother is suggestive and requires investigation. And his link with the Snakenborg Gallery could tie him in with the murder there, too.'

Gray nodded agreement and the two men, kindred spirits in the art, science and Mechanick Exercise of quiet contemplation, lapsed into an easy silence which might have lasted until judgement day, or at least until Gray's didactic duties intervened, had not a wobble-creak-wobble and a general commotion announced the entrance of Miss Gemima Malherbie, the cleaner, on her diurnal journey around Em Quad. She was a broad, though comely, woman of some forty summers (and, presumably, a concomitant number of winters). She was, if the Isleworth grapevine was to be trusted,[173] as they said in the argo of a previous age, 'no better than she ought'. Had Gray heard the gossip or noticed her rather pretty

173 Which it should *not,* on moral nor evidentiary grounds. The University's bush telegraph is as vicious instrument of intimidation as the Cheka or Mugabe's Central Intelligence Organisation.

face, he might have found her presence rather unsettling. As it was, he found her presence only mildly irritating. He was very susceptible to female beauty, but only on the very rare occasions on which he noticed it, as was the case with Miss (or rather *Doctor*) Datt. Fortunately, both the Professor and Miss Malherbie were oblivious to any potential danger which lurked below the surface of their working relationship. She was too busy attempting to suppress the dust which seemed to accumulate more rapidly in the Professor's rooms than elsewhere; he, too, seemed almost permanently pre-occupied with these fugs, these small particles of homeless and abandoned matter. Was their preponderance related to the second law of thermodynamics? Since his understanding of physics was of a very elementary nature, he had little hope of discovering the answer to this question.

As Miss Malherbie did what little she could to stem the rising tide of dust upon the Professor's desk, Clanarsh dozed on the stuffing-exuding sofa and Gray thrummed a drum solo upon the arm of his chair. Eventually, Miss Malherbie left and an unusual calm descended upon the study. At least, until a medium-calibre rifle bullet penetrated a fifteenth-century diamond-shaped pane of glass a few inches from Gray's head with almost murderous efficiency. Although unharmed, Gray was furious. A number of the window panes had been replaced over the years, especially in the late eighteenth century. Those modern usurpers, he felt, detracted from the antiquarian charm of the whole window – possibly the whole building; they were too smooth, too colourless, too free from bubbles and foreign bodies. Now another ancient pane would have to be replaced, in all probability by glass of even less character than the Georgian variety, possibly even from a sheet created by the Pilkington float glass method.[174] He felt sick at the thought – and sick again at the thought that the bullet might have buried itself in one of the venerable beams from which his rooms were constructed. All

---

174 Floating on a bed of molten tin is hardly character-forming in glass terms.

this occurred to him before Clanarsh showed any sign of awakening from his slumbers.

Although the detective gave some minor indications that he might be about to rouse himself after the intrusion of the rifle bullet, he soon relapsed into a gentle sleep and Gray decided to hunt for the projectile before disturbing him. He glanced at the window which had, through no fault of its own, allowed its ingress. Surprisingly, perhaps, the pane, which college accounts indicate had been new in 1473, had not shattered. Gray wondered (without great enthusiasm) if the round hole at its centre could be filled with plastic resin, in the manner of windscreen repairs. The leading had been pushed in slightly, a very easy thing to fix. He also noticed that the pane was thicker at the bottom than the top. He had once believed the old wives' tale that glass, being an amorphous solid, flowed slowly down, leaving old windows wedge-shaped, and wished he still believed it.[175] Some myths are consoling. These observations being not entirely germane to his search for the bullet, Gray let them loose to float about the room with the dust while he estimated the height of the hole from the floor – about 6′ 4″ – and distance from the right-hand study wall – perhaps 17′ – and then looked at the corresponding area of the rear wall. At first he saw nothing, but scanning the wall slowly from right to left (like reading Hebrew or Arabic, he thought), he saw the dull glint of brass between a vertical timber[176] and the lime-washed plaster (mud, cow-dung and horse-hair smoothed lovingly onto wooden laths). Restrained rather by a concern for the building's fabric than for police procedure, he decided to leave the projectile *in situ* for a scene of crime officer from the appropriate authority, which, unfortunately, was the Isleworth University Constabulary. There was no ambiguity of jurisdiction. And yet...

---

175   Medieval glass was of uneven thickness and it was only natural to place the thicker part at the bottom. Even so, there is no statistical evidence that old windows are thicker at the bottom than the top.

176   Or what passed for vertical to the average Isleworth builder, circa 1390.

Gray scanned the surrounding buildings It was clear that the shot had been fired from the opposite side of the quadrangle at approximately the same height as his study, perhaps Professor Delauney's rooms. It was a perfect platform for an attempted assassination (if that was what it was), as Herriott Delauney's academic career had been marked more by his absences than his presence. The Professor of Romance (or more correctly Dobray Professor of Romance Languages and Literature) was so called because he was strikingly handsome and much admired, not to say desired, by his female colleagues and students.[177]

As well as being handsome, Delauney, like Gray, was a great believer in the conservation of energy, even if he approached it in a more vigorous manner, attending all manner of conferences with abstruse and dull-sounding titles in comfortable or interesting places: Cambridge (both the English one, which seems exotic to the denizens of Isleworth, and the Massachusetts variety, which does not) Biarritz, Shuzhou, Naples, Barcelona, Rio,[178] Sintra, Aspen, Hangzhou, Chamonix, Lausanne. Never Bucharest, Chicago, Detroit, Birmingham (well, possibly the real one, but never its upstart cousin in Alabama) or Shenzhen. When Gray had remarked in passing about his unofficial title, Delauney had replied. 'Oh, I'm sure you are mistaken, Gerrish. They probably said "Professor of Romansch," which I suppose I am, *inter alia*.' It was a rather long speech for Delauney and it left him rather enervated for a day or two.

Gray, reluctantly deciding that it was time to rouse Chief Inspector Clanarsh (whom we are inclined, in our foolish fashion, to christen 'Clanarsh of the Yard') from his slumbers, gave the man a gentle prod in the ribs. The detective stirred slowly, like a stew coming to a simmer over a low heat; his sleep was deep and sedimentary. The merest hint of a smile played on his lips and Gray

---

177 I hope to discuss Delauney's life in more detail at a future date, in another case investigated by the Snakeborg Professor. It may well be entitled *The Professor of Romance*.
178 Did that place name always conjure up for him as it did for Gray the Fred Astair film, *Flying Down to Rio*, with girls dancing on the wings of planes?

wondered what, if anything occupied his dreams. He didn't really want to know and so he administered a rather harsher summons to Clanarsh's outstretched shin which, despite some protection afforded by tweed trousering, produced the desired effect. The detective's head arched right in a sudden spasm and his arms propelled him from the sofa to a standing position with remarkable speed. 'Grumph!' he announced to the world, and opened his bleary eyes. 'Sorry, I seem to have dozed off, Prof.'

If Gray was surprised to be thus addressed by an officer of the Metropolitan Police, he did not show it.

'You missed the fun,' he said, pointing to the perforated window. 'This old glass is irreplaceable,' he added sadly and then gave Clanarsh a précis of recent events.

27: A Bull in a China Shop

The bull, of himself, is well enough, and may indeed be a highly respectable animal in his own place and way; but in a china shop his presence is highly unsuitable, and likely to prove most disastrous.[179]

I T NOW SEEMED inevitable that the Isleworth Bulls would be involved in the investigation of the shooting; in the end, Gray accepted that and phoned the Police Station. While he waited for a representative of that constabulary to arrive, he tried to think of some way to have the case transferred to the Met.

Clanarsh was looking rather sheepish, either from embarrassment at having slept through the murderous assault or because he was trespassing on another force's 'manor'.

Gray made some more coffee.

What neither man had anticipated was the spectacle which would present itself when the full majesty of the law was visited upon them. At first there was a low rumble like a gathering storm, then an unprecedented series of wobble-creep-wobbles, culminating in a thunderous crash on the massive oaken door as surely no human fist could have made.

Gray opened the door timidly to reveal the very substantial presence of Vortimer Williams in full dress uniform of early Victorian design, carrying his large brass mace of office which, it was clear, had been used to herald his entrance. Other than being royal blue, the uniform could almost have belonged to a Bow Street Runner, or at least a Peeler. Two rows of large brass buttons ran down the tunic, which was cinched at the waist by an ornately-buckled belt, fitting so tightly that the impression was of a well-coopered barrel. A long sword dangled from the belt in a jaunty naval fashion,

---

179 James Miller, *Nephalism: True Temperance or Scripture Science, and Experience,* Glasgow: Scottish Temperance League, [nd], p. 10.

perhaps influenced by the sabres once worn by Swedish police officers. The lower portion of the Proctor's ample figure was encased in snuggly-fitting white trousers and high-gloss riding boots. His pudgy hands were disguised by the most elegant and delicate white kid gloves. His left hand gripped a grotesque Pickelhaube[180] ornamented with the University's arms in brass. Oh, I forgot to mention his short cape, the underside of which was lined with saffron silk, intricately woven with the emblems of his office – a bull, Hercules wielding a gnarled club, an owl and the lamp of learning.

'What have you been up to, Professor Gray?' boomed the magisterial presence.

'Someone took a pot-shot at the window,' Gray replied pointing to the damaged pane; 'Some student prank, no doubt.'

'Are you telling me that I have been delayed in attending an important luncheon for the Association of Chief Police Officers to investigate a hoax?'

'Er, it would seem so. I'm sorry, Vortimer. I didn't request your presence. I assumed a constable would come.'

'Well, while I'm here I'd better take a look,' said Williams grudgingly. He drew a small magnifying glass (little more than a linen-tester) from an inside pocket and examined the hole in the window pane.

'A small hole probably made by a BB pellet,' he pronounced.

Gray did not feel obliged to draw his attention to the rifle bullet, and the Proctor left for his ACPO luncheon without further ado.

---

180 Some might describe it as a Custodian helmet, but it was distinguished from the normal bobby's headwear in that it was surmounted by a substantial and vicious-looking spike. Note also that unlike a normal Custodian helmet, its fittings were of brass and its badge was not contained within a Brunswick star.

28: The Smoking Gun

CLANARSH MIGHT HAVE resented being completely over-looked under different circumstances, but both he and Gray were relieved by the perfunctory nature of the Proctor's investigation. They felt absolved from giving the Bulls any further information, at least for the present.

'We'd better go and look for the shooter's vantage point,' said Gray. 'Oh, by the way, the bullet's over here.'

Clanarsh donned gloves and teased the large brass object from its dense oak coffin with a pair of tweezers, slipping it into a small manilla bag. Clearly, he always came prepared. 'Looks like a 7.62 by 51 mm NATO round. It's going to be difficult to fudge the paperwork, but I'll run it through our lab. We'll have some major explaining to do if it matches the one which killed Yllingstone.'

Gray nodded, 'Now let's get across the quadrangle.' The buildings on that side, completed in 1483, bore some resemblance to Oxford's Divinity School, being in the Late Perpendicular style. Gray pushed open a great oak door and ran up two flights of stone steps to the second floor, followed closely by the man from the Met. He rapped on Delauney's room but received no reply.

'You might wish to avert your eyes,' said Gray. The detective grinned and turned to study a rather plain piece of fifteen-century masonry.

With a few deft clicks of the pick-locks the door swung open and the two men entered Delauney's rooms. One thing struck Gray immediately: the lack of dust. The rooms had not been occupied for weeks but looked perfectly clean. Being late fifteenth century (new in Isleworth terms), they were more spacious and lighter than Gray's. Everything was very neat. Gray stepped over to the large study windows. If the sniper had fired from here, he would have needed to open one of the three central panels. The dust-free environment meant that detecting any disturbance was difficult.

'I don't suppose you brought any fingerprint powder with you?' he asked, but Clanarsh shook his head sadly. Clearly he was not as well-prepared as Gray had previously thought.

'Never mind. I'm sure our man was far too careful to leave prints,' Gray said, flinging open the centremost window. 'Well, I think we have our smoking gun. The outer frame, which is covered by the window when closed, is slightly wet while its companions on either side are dry. You'll remember that it was raining earlier.'

'Hardly conclusive proof. Perhaps the cleaner opened it.'

'Perhaps,' said Gray, 'But Mrs Malherbie is not a great one for opening windows. Well, I'm afraid there are no clues here.'

'Except, Gerrish, that it must have been someone who knew the rooms would be empty and had a key – or picked the lock! Some-one who is pretty familiar with the University in general.'

'That's a rather large field, sighed Gray. He scanned the room, from the maroon carpet to the (incongruously modern) Jacobean plasterwork of the ceiling, across to the small kitchen with its gran-ite work surfaces and induction hob. He glanced in the bathroom and rummaged through the garments on the coat rack by the front door.

Clanarsh kept his hands in his trouser pockets and looked about uneasily. 'Do you do this sort of thing often?' he asked.

'No, not often,' replied the Professor, examining the contents of a desk drawer. 'Sheraton. A bit effeminate for my taste, but the work-manship is superb. Those crisp little dovetail joints...' He went into the small bedroom but did not linger there.

'The gunman must have opened the window and then lain down on the desk,' he continued. 'The depth of the desk is only about four and a half feet, so we're either dealing with someone very short or he must have rested his lower legs on something about the same height as the desk.'

Clanarsh looked around. The general neatness of the room was an advantage.

'I noticed as we came in that this chair was a couple of inches further from the door than its pair,' he said.

'Ah, and that cushion,' said Gray, 'The one on the sofa. It's less perfectly plumped than the other two. One could rest one's legs on the chair back, with the cushion in-between for comfort. It's not ideal but an experienced sniper could use such an arrangement. And it's not very far – only two hundred, two hundred and fifty metres.'

'And he missed,' Clanarsh pointed out.

'If he or she meant to hit. Do you think it is worth sending the cushion to your forensic lab for minute examination?'

'I suppose so,' Clanarsh said without enthusiasm. 'God knows what I'll tell the Super. We need something to pack it in.'

Gray went into the kitchen and came back shortly with a swing-bin liner. 'I don't suppose this will contaminate it too much.'

Clanarsh agreed and the left, Gray relocking the door on the way out.

'I'll send Herriott a note about the missing cushion,' he said.

29: The Archbishop at Home

Ye shall understand that my quartane[181] hath so much distempered the state of my health, that without apparent danger I cannot as yet commit myself to accept the great honour which the right worshipful Sir William Cecil, secretary to the Queen's majesty, is desirous to confer upon me.[182]

A LIGHT WENT ON in Lambeth Palace and the Most Reverend and Right Honorable Samson Gostrey, one-hundred-and-somethingth Archbishop of Canterbury, Primate of All England and Metropolitan, stepped into his steaming bath. After a few misunderstandings about his time in the gambling industry, his rise in the Church of England had been meteoric – he'd barely been a bishop for about three years before ascending the archiepiscopal throne – and he was still having a little difficulty coming to terms with some of the more bizarre aspects of the job. Harrow, Magdalene (Cambridge, as indicated by what Oxonians would regard as a superfluous e), Tesco, William Hill and the Church of England itself could not prepare him for everything. Only yesterday, he had received an invitation from the Vice-Chancellor of a university he'd never heard of to an event called a waysgoose – a word unfamiliar to him.[183] The invitation itself was no mere die-stamped flimflammery with gilded edges. It was a fully-fledged parchment which began:

To the Right Reverend Father in God, my Lord, the Archbishop of Canterbury, his Grace, Metropolitan and Primate of All England, the Fellows, Masters, Graduates, Undergraduates, Officers and Servants of the University of Isleworth in the County of Middlesex pray for his long Continuance

---

181 Malaria.
182 An extract of a letter from Matthew Parker to Sir Nicholas Bacon, August 1558. Parker MSS. C. C. Coll. Camb. CVI. art. 304. p.743. Parker is referring to the Vice-Chancellorship of Isleworth. Had illness not prevented him accepting the post, he might never have become Archbishop of Canterbury. But who is to say which honour is the greater?
183 A fact which surely points to a deficiency in the Cambridge educational system.

of Health, both in Body and Soul, to the Glory of God, and the whole Body of the Church, and the Congregation of all good Christians and all other Persons of whatever Faith...

The calligraphy was excellent but surely the whole thing was over the top for a party invitation? To add to his perplexity, he'd noticed that the franking on the cardboard tube (he always opened his own post – a precaution which had been essential in his gambling industry days) proclaimed Isleworth to be Britain's oldest university. Could this be true? He sank into the warm, sudsy water (courtesy of Badedas) and decided to ask the Palace's Librarian, Giles Mandelbrote, a small, bespectacled man of startling erudition. If anyone would know, Giles would (even if he had gone to the 'other' university – and he didn't mean Isleworth). Come to think of it, hadn't he seen something about the University of Isleworth in Matthew Parker's correspondence? Sadly, few of the original letters were to hand at Lambeth, being mainly at Corpus Christi (Cambridge), but he had the 1853 printed volume somewhere – he'd ask Alex if she'd seen it. Had he left it in the downstairs loo with his own *Gambling for God* and a Dick Francis given to him at Frankfurt Airport by Rabbi Lionel Blue? His yellow rubber duck[184] floated inexorably towards him, oblivious to soap suds or human cares.

---

184 I say rubber for reasons of convention, but, as you have probably surmised, it was made from a synthetic polymer. Why 'rubber' ducks should invariably be yellow is one of life's abiding mysteries and one which perhaps Professor Gray will care to elucidate when he can spare a month or two for research.

30: Isleworth Madonna

THE SNAKENBORG GALLERY, much of its interior faced in fiery red Ruabon brick, was looking at its most magnificent and Gray kept seeing new features in Waterhouse's architecture which he had not noticed before – the terracotta ravens (or possibly they were Cornish chuffs) which flanked the upper corners of the door lintels and the gaudily-glazed tiles which subverted the Doric order of the columns in the main gallery. Most remarkable were the unglazed encaustic floor tiles whose motifs encompassed the fruiterer's art and the black science of greengrocery[185] – onions, carrots, potatoes, chard, a pyramid of Brussels sprouts, beetroots, spinach, cauliflowers, lettuces, tomatoes, pineapples, Seville oranges and purple flowering broccoli were all represented. Despite this superabundance of decoration, the Gallery somehow managed to avoid the showy vulgarity of the same architect's National Liberal Club. Gray was particularly taken by the national flowers of the United kingdom as re-interpreted by Waterhouse (or some unidentified minion): the rose of England was replaced with an Black Isleworth Pine Strawberry (which is a fellow member of the Rosaceae family), the Welsh daffodil was dropped for the more edible and equally Welsh emblem of the leek and Scotland's thistle was represented by the globe artichoke (which, as any donkey will tell you, is nothing but a large thistle). Ireland's shamrock was replaced with watercress, perhaps relying on a vague similarity in appearance or the saintly Edmund Campion's claim about the Irish that, 'Shamrotes, watercresses, rootes, and other herbes they feed upon.'[186] It has been said, by Pevsner amongst others, that the

---

185   Which had, after all, financed this most exuberant of all Victorian buildings.

186   In James Ware (ed.), *The historie of Ireland collected by three learned authors, viz. Meredith Hanmer Doctor in Divinitie, Edmund Campion sometime fellow of St Iohns Colledge in Oxford, and Edmund Spenser Esq.*, Dublin: printed by the Societie of Stationers, printers to the Kings most excellent Majestie [and London: by Thomas Harper], 1633.

Gallery incorporates design elements developed by Waterhouse for Strangeways Prison in Manchester. As a law-abiding academic who seldom felt any need to travel West of Oxford or North of Cambridge, Gray did not feel equipped to make an informed rebuttal of this supposition.

The group consisted of Dr Behr (the Vice-Chancellor), Miss Datt, Tim Hutchisson from the Courtauld, Marietta Snakenborg, Esther Dalhousie, Big Dave Trentwistle (the Gallery Curator), Gray (hastily discarding his bicycle clips) and, last but no means least, the vast, rubicund figure of Charlton Mitchelberger, freshly belched Jonah-like from the swollen belly of a superjumbo, in a wrinkled seersucker suit of doubtful provenance. I was not invited; there is no place for poets in an art gallery, as Arthtur Koestler once remarked. An unpleasant man, but he was right about that. They climbed the broad marble staircase, past the Archimboldos which captured the greengrocering spirit of the Snakenborg Collection so precisely, to the upper gallery. Mitchelberger, once he had recovered his breath, waddled over to the Madonna, dwarfing it in both height and breadth and depriving it of light, while signally failing to eclipse its beauty. He peered deeply into its craquelure, blew into a man-sized silk handkerchief adorned with pink and navy blue spots and, much to Gray's surprise and disappointment, burst out laughing – a resonant cackle worthy of even the most self-respecting hell-hound.

'Damn it, Professor Gray, you didn't expect me to fall for that did you?'

Whereas the American had been merely loathsome before, he had become in Gray's mind positively demonic and he bit back a response.

'You are questioning its authenticity, Professor Mitchelberger?' asked Behr, nervously.

'No,' boomed Mitchelberger, 'I am not questioning its authenticity. There is no question that it is a fake and equally no question that Professor Gray knows it is. It's not even painted on a wooden panel, for heaven's sake; it's on what looks like MDF to me and I'd bet my last dollar that it's painted in acrylics.'

'Haha,' said Gray without conviction, 'Just a little joke. It's not really a fake. Just a student's practice piece. We, er, had to leave it here while we took the original away for closer examination.'

'Where's the original, Gerrish?' snapped the Vice-Chancellor; 'I hope you haven't lost it.'

'Oh, it's safe. In the Courtauld Institute.'

'Hold on,' said Big Dave (who was in on the 'joke'), 'You can't just walk off with one of our paintings without permission, or even *with* permission for that matter. It's a breach of the terms of the bequest, Section 3.1 – "Should any painting, sculpture or other work of art be removed from the oversight of the Curator or Curators of the said Collection, the Bequest is deemed void..."' His ample muscles flexed menacingly under the inadequate cover of his rugby shirt's blue and purple stripes (the colour of Isleworth's First XV).[187]

'We'll have to worry about that later,' said Gray. 'I had to get it tested and that wasn't possible here.'

'There's still the little matter of the Eiffel Tower, Professor Gray,' remarked Mitchelberger, rather over-egging the drawl of his native Virginia.

'I's not the Eiffel Tower, it's the Crystal Palace Television Transmitter,' Gray said decisively, as though this fact alone was enough to confirm the painting's place in the canon of Italian Renaissance art.

'Well it damn well looks like the Eiffel Tower to me,' said Mitchelberger who had never visited Paris but had once seen a postcard of the Tower's simulacrum at Las Vegas, 'And no television transmitter's going to convince me that it's a genuine Raphael. What's

---

187 Fifteen is actually an arbitrary number. Isleworth plays what, amongst the vulgar throng, is known as Stonehenge Rugby. It is largely deficient in rules (the only one I remember is 'no weapons') and the size of teams varies according to availability. Although some attempt is made to balance the numbers on opposing teams, it is not unheard of for six or seven to take on as many as seventeen. Courtesy usually dictates that the smaller team wins.

this Crystal Palace business, anyway? You still have crystal sets in this country?'

'The area is called Crystal Palace after the glass structure constructed in Hyde Park to contain the Great Exhibition of 1851,' said Gray. 'It was relocated to Sydenham Hill in 1854 and burnt down in 1936, but the name stuck. There are still some charming, if inaccurate, model dinosaurs around there, though.'

'So it postdates Raphael by more than 330 years,' observed Mitchelberger.

'That is, of course, true, but there's more to it. I think you'll be interested.'

'Well, I'd certainly be interested to see this Crystal Palace,' said Mitchelberger sourly. 'It's just a pity is burnt down more than seventy-five years ago. I bet it would have been rather dusty by now. I've seen what some of your public buildings look like. No-one ever cleans the glass. I'm not surprised it burnt down. All that dust building up's got to be flammable.'

Gray was about to reply waspishly but thought better of it when he remembered all the dust in his study, those delicate particles circling and descending slowly to the floor with hypnotic insouciance. He was somewhat surprised that Mitchelberger seemed to share his interest in the subject.

'Anyway,' Tim Hutchisson butted in, 'Professor Gray and I have some very interesting findings which we'd like to share with you. It's a sort of historical detective story. We really need to hurry if we're going to catch the train.'

'The train!' said Mitchelberger, aghast at such an old-fashioned form of transportation. He imagined what they looked like in Hicksville, Middlesex – antiquated coal-burning contraptions with cow-catchers at the front. Even Professor Mitchelberger had heard of the famous Isleworth cattle and did not doubt their ability to fell even the mightiest iron horse.

'I'm afraid it's a little walk to Syon Lane Station,' said Gray.

'Don't you have cars over here?' asked Mitchelberger sourly, although, as he'd arrived from Heathrow in a black cab, he knew the answer.

'It's quicker to walk,' Gray replied. 'We had our own line in the old days – an "atmospheric railway" constructed by the Samuda Brothers in the 1840s. The station is still there behind those trees. Unfortunately, the rats used to gnaw the leather flanges. It never worked very well. The line ran more or less under our feet to Kew Bridge. Perhaps they'll reopen it one day. It would be very handy.' Although, as he said these words, a ghastly vision of Isleworth thronging with tourists crept into his mind.

Natives of Isleworth will know well the pleasant, tree-lined path from the University to Syon Lane Station but it will mean little to outsiders, so I'll say no more about the journey to the Courtauld Institute or the subsequent revelations until a later chapter where it will make more sense.

31: The Man with the Umbrella

IT WAS ABOUT this time, a few days before the Waysgoose, that Professor Gray told me he was going to Cambridge. To be honest, I was rather shocked. Although an alumnus of that rival institution myself, I have long since learnt to treat it and Oxford with the same level of disdain as is affected by other Isleworthian academics. Gray, of course, has his own code of conduct, but I was nonetheless surprised.

He was gone (and this is almost inevitable given the failings of the railway network between civilization and Cambridge) for many hours. On his return he looked tired and yet elated and invited me to accompany him to the Garden of Earthly Delights where, sitting in the garden as the sun sank, he told me of his travels. Indeed, his narrative was almost entirely about the travelling rather than the arriving, and even less about the purpose and outcome of his visit, so forgive me if my own account is similarly unbalanced.

His journey had a certain symmetry. He started, for some unfathomable reason, at Brentford station (a modest Victorian building which lost its charm, like many others, when it was modernsed), where signs informed Professor Gray that he was at the home of the West London University.[188] Crossing the Thames at Barnes, he travelled in an easterly direction to Vauxhall (former home of the famous pleasure gardens and now home of the Secret Intelligence Service – although, like so much of this story, that is irrelevant) whence he was conveyed northward by Victoria Line (which, unlike much of the Tube network, is not Victorian) to that handsome Victorian terminus, King's Cross Station, now reinvented in glass and steel. An ugly and rather uncomfortable train of the ubiquitous type then transported him, if not to the heart of Cambridge (because the station is banished in donnish fashion to the outskirts

---

188 Why *the* West London University? There are other West London universities, including my own.

of the ancient city), to a Victorian suburb of the same. Cambridge, Gray learnt from a sign not dissimilar to that at Brentford was the home of Anglia Ruskin University, rather Gray thought, in the manner that Schlitz is said to be the beer that made Milwaukee famous; he was grateful for this insight, although I need hardly say that he has no idea where Milwaukee is and neither (forgive me Milwaukeeans!) have I.

He could, in theory, have brought his Brompton on the journey but, despite its many virtues, he found it rather heavy to carry on the public transport system, and so he needed another mode of transport for the final leg. Since, in any case, he was in no hurry,[189] he chose to catch neither the bus nor a taxi, but to walk. Judging from the detail which he provided of his journey (of which only the essentials are provided here), I can only suppose that he walked in a slow and contemplative fashion as befits a 'foreign' don in Cambridge.[190]

He strode (for which read 'ambled') down Station Road with its crammers, schools of English and an outpost of the Open University, turning right on Hills Road with its modest Victorian buildings and hideous HSBC, the uninspired Terrington House and the high Victorian vulgarity of the Church of Our Lady and the English Martyrs. Crossing Gonville Place, with its thoroughly reprehensible Lloyds Bank,[191] he found himself rather closer to the ancient heart of the city and with Hills Road transubstantiated into Regent Street. He passed several Greene King pubs which he

189 It is a trait I much admire in Professor Gray that he is seldom if ever in a hurry.
190 See the late Richard Feynman's unpublished description of his 1986 visit to Cambridge to deliver the Dirac Lecture – Isleworth University Library, Feynmann-371002.P. His impromptu performance on the bongo drums at the Pitt Building had unexpected and long-lasting consequences for Cambridge University Press and is blamed by some, though not by me, for the demise of its printing division. No doubt this will continue to be a subject for scholarly debate but I have checked the records and I can see no evidence that he gave a similar performance in Oxford in the decades before Oxford University Press closed its printing division in 1989.
191 I speak architecturally, for the perceptive student will observe the building's remarkable resemblance to one of those *Blue Peter* projects in which young children are unwisely encouraged to produce something – say for argument's sake a multistorey carpark – out of cereal packets.

seemed to remember had been Tolly Cobbold houses in his youth. And what had happened to Rayments?[192]

He passed the handsome neoclassical façade of Downing College and the utterly hideous University Arms. Past the unknapped flint of St Andrew's Street Baptist Church (two girls taking a fag break on the steps) he strode (ambled), past the acceptable if rather dull façade of Emmanuel – ah, what tales he could tell of *that* college![193] When he came to the fantastical armorial above the gate to Christ's, he knew he had arrived in the 'real' Cambridge,[194] although whether that was a good thing or not, he did not know. He passed Sydney Sussex, the Round Church and St John's but where exactly he went after that I cannot tell you. That is, I know he went to see the Master of Waterman's but, although I was both an undergraduate and postgraduate at Cambridge, I have never knowingly seen that college. It is, I understand from Professor Gray, a college which like Isleworth shuns the limelight. It is, he says, modest but not obscure, with no open gateway manned by a porter; instead there is what looks like a domestic doorway and you must ring the bell to be admitted. I imagine that it is one of those anonymous buildings one passes, a narrow town house which fronts a larger and more magnificent set of collegiate buildings.[195] It boasts among its alumni Sir Randolph Summersby (late of the Foreign and Commonwealth Office) and Millicent Behr (*née* Hughes-Abernathy).

The Master, he tells me, is a petite blonde, a former High Court judge 'of the better sort' whom he had known since they were both in their early thirties.

---

192   I am frankly astounded by Professor Gray's ignorance of the matter. This majestic brewery in Furneux Pelham was closed by Greene King in 1987.

193   And I urge him to do so, although there are undoubtedly 'Emma' alumni who hope that he will keep these to himself.

194   After all, he was within yards of Heffers which had promised to stock *A Short History of the Letter K* as soon as the final volume was published. Even so, he rather wondered if he wanted to be stocked by a bookshop which had long dropped its apostrophe.

195   Anyone who likes doors disguised as bookcases (and who does not?) must surely admire such an arrangement, especially if it deters tourists.

'It's The Man with the Umbrella!' she exclaimed enthusiastically as he entered her dark and cosy study.[196]

After catching up on old times while drinking what Gray considered rather flavourless tea from the finest Meissen cups, he touched upon the reason for his visit, Millicent Hughes-Abernathy.

'She was an undergraduate here when I was doing my best to become a perpetual student, second doctorate, that sort of nonsense,' said the Master of Waterman's, pouring them another cup of tea. 'Would you like a chocolate Hobnob? I think I have some somewhere. She was a rather serious girl, I think, but I only knew her through the Toxophily Society. She was a keen riflewoman, too, but I always think guns are boys' toys. Rather vulgar. She was a first-rate archer – could have been a world champion, which makes what happened even more unfortunate. She seems to have been dogged with bad luck.'

Declining the Hobnob, Gray urged her to continue.

'She had two boyfriends that I remember. The first was Dennis, er, Freeman, I think. A sweet boy. Studied Chemistry, too, which is how they met. He joined the Toxophily Society mostly to spend more time with her, I suspect, but he was quite good and seemed to enjoy it.'

She shuddered slightly and continued. 'No-one seems to know exactly what happened. He was found dying in the wood at the edge of the archery field.'

'He was shot?'

'Shot? No, oh, I see, you thought perhaps a stray arrow... No. There were no wounds. He just died. The postmortem came up with no real explanation. His lips were cyanosed, he had vomitted. It looked like poison but nothing was ever found in his system. He and Millicent had had an argument and it was suggested that he

---

196   This was, he tells me, her usual greeting to him, owing to the fact (long withheld from me and other close associates) that in his youth he had appeared as an extra in a long-forgotten British New Wave film. Much to his surprise, the producers actually listed him in the credits as playing 'Man with Umbrella'. It was undoubtedly the high point of his cinematic career.

[141]

committed suicide – but it was just a suggestion. The inquest re-corded an open verdict. And then there was Henry... Henry Vine, I think his name was. They went on a camping holiday together in Dorset or somewhere. She woke up one morning and he'd gone. Fallen off a cliff, apparently, of which there are a lot in Dorset, if that's where it was. So, there you are; the poor young thing lost two boyfriends in her undergraduate years. Wretched.'

The Master of Waterman's broke off and dabbed her eyes dain-tily.

And that, I'm afraid, is all Gray told me at the time of his visit to Cambridge. I only discovered the outcome of his investigation later and I shall leave this revelation nestled deeply in the appropriate chronology.

32: Teddy Behr's Picnic

If you go down in the woods today you're sure of a big surprise.[197]

'Anton de Moresco is a poet with his metre running.'[198]

THE PARTY, AN informal one, set off for the woods in little bunches of three or four, ambling, chattering. Many of the men wore white or cream linen suits and Panama hats and carried bags, baskets or hampers filled with food and drink, while the women mostly wore light cotton dresses and broad-brimmed hats. Chummy Beetleson's suit was of coarse-textured, pale celadon Shangtung silk and was accompanied by an off-white, open-necked cotton shirt. Professor Mitchelberger wore a white seersucker suit with light blue stripe and carried a Fortnum & Mason hamper. Their path was strewn (by nature rather than artifice) with flowers – common figwort, agrimony, common centaury, bittersweet, enchanter's nightshade, nipplewort, creeping jenny, creeping cinquefoil, wild angelica, together with other plants which grow in Isleworth alone and whose names I do not know. Small animals scuttled, leapt, hopped or ran through the undergrowth; birds sang from every branch, and a gentle breeze urged the canopy to animate the dappling of all flora and fauna beneath it, including the waysgoosers.

Sadly the Archbishop of Canterbury (who, after consulting Alex, Giles and various theological and historical authorities, had concluded that a waysgoose at England's oldest university was not something to be despised) genuinely regretted that he could not come, not that anyone expected such a visitation; only two archbishops had ever attended the waysgoose, Rowan Williams and Reginald Pole. Williams had incurred Dr Behr's wrath by saying

---

197   *The Teddy Bears' Picnic,* lyrics by Jimmy Kennedy.
198   Michael Panjellicum, Director, Poetry Research Institute, University of Leeds.

grace before the meal ('far too pious for a bearded lefty') while Pole, who was not invited to the waysgoose in 1556 but turned up anyway, was widely despised in Isleworth for his enthusiastic incineration of protestants (notably John Hall, Vicar of Isleworth) under the revival of the Heresy Acts.[199] It is for this reason that the Guy on the Isleworth University bonfire every 5 November wears a red cardinal's hat. That Pole had convinced Bloody Mary to refound the Monastery of Syon, with the concomitant loss of valuable University lands, was another black mark against his name and the fact that Pole had served as Vice-Chancellor of both Cambridge and Oxford Universities only added to Isleworthian distaste.

I attended the waysgoose myself, in an *ex officio* capacity, ambling along near the back of this disjointed crocodile with Professor Gray,[200] my presence being required for the reading of my newly-composed ode to St Bride. Unfortunately, the identity of St Bride is somewhat confused in the collective Isleworth imagination. The printers, who were, after all, the presiding geniuses of the waysgoose (and possibly of very aspect of the University), believed her to be St Bridget of Ireland who gave her name to the printers' Church off Fleet Street, while the academics[201] tended to favour St Bridget of Sweden whose nuns used to frolic in the water meadows of Syon. As a poet, I remain fastidiously neutral on the matter.

'It's a pity Merlin can't be here,' said Gray; 'He always enjoys it. We have some of his cider and apple brandy, though,' he added, lifting one of the massive stoneware flagons he was carrying. 'He'll be here in spirit.'

---

199   (1 & 2 Ph. & M. c.6).

200   I need hardly say that we were both properly attired in off-white linen suits. Gray wore a silk bow-tie hand-painted with the University arms, I a Balliol tie (to which I had no claim), a vulgar confection with multiple instances of the college arms embroidered rather badly by machine in polyester. Gray's hat was a Panama of the old school, while I wore a boater jauntily cocked to one side, its band gaily striped in blue, white and red (azure, argent and goules if you wish to be pedantic).

201   I do not intend here to draw a false dichotomy between printers and academics. Many printers are also academics, in a broad sense of the word.

Literally, I thought. The baroque band and singers who accompanied us, resplendent in their eighteenth-century brocaded coats, struck up a Handel air, which was beautiful but inimical to composing the final verse of my ode which lay uncompleted in a dusty recess of my brain. I, too, missed Merlin. It had been his influence as a fellow poet (he was, and still is, a name to be conjured with on the Eisteddfod circuit, despite being – at most – one quarter Welsh), intermingled with that of several quarts of Double Elephant, which had transformed me from a rather dull lecturer in Middle English Literature (is there any other sort of lecturer on the subject?) into what was, until the late nineteenth century, known simply as the Master of Poetry; it is a title I prefer to the present one, not least because of its implied mastery of technique.

We stumbled (almost literally, despite not having broached the apple brandy) upon the ruins of the Norman chapel dedicated to St Eulalia of Mérida in a small clearing, which earlier in the year had been covered in bluebells. I was reminded of the poem:

> Buona pulcella fut eulalia.
> Bel auret corps bellezour anima.

It always seemed a rather bouncy beginning to a rather horrible tale, and you could say the same for the early stages of our waysgoose. By now the band was playing a hornpipe by Purcell and this jaunty tune propelled us deeper into the darkness of the woods which echoed with the hammering of woodpeckers, the crawing of jays and the soft cooing of wood pigeons. Last autumn's leaf litter rattled at our feet.

Eventually, we arrived at our destination, a far larger clearing which was kept in suitable condition to host the annual waysgoose by judicious felling. Many of the party spread rugs on the ground while others sat on tree stumps, erected folding chairs or, like Chummy, Gerrish and myself, sat on logs. The clearing was large enough that the centre was completely unshaded from the sun, so we were glad to take a large log on the periphery which enjoyed some gentle dappling from the tall oaks, beeches and hornbeams around us.

Proceedings were opened by Ray Clench, Printer to the University,[202] who called for a toast to Dr and Mrs Behr. This was really an error, as Millicent had a DPhil herself (albeit from some lesser institution, but the toast rang out. 'Dr and Mrs Behr,' which made me think of Goldilocks. Gray poured himself a stiff apple brandy while Beetleson opened a bottle of that old favourite among Isleworth dons,[203] raspberry wine,[204] which he poured carelessly into a Georgian glass with air-twist stem, where it lay prettily, but not for long. Throughout the clearing the masses helped themselves or others to various wines, ciders, beers and spirits but I contented myself, *pro tem,* with ginger beer, conscious of my poetical obligations. As game birds, watercress, lettuces, tomatoes, tabouleh, scotch eggs, falafels, smoked trout, sill matjes (as always served with potato salad), pork pies, game pies, langoustines with homemade mayonnaise, slices of tortilla, cold roast beef, hard-boiled quails' eggs, lobsters, crayfish, samosas, pakoras, dolmades, jellied eels, smoked salmon, rocket leaves, radicchio, peppers green and red, crabs, cucumbers, avocados and ham sandwiches with English mustard were unwrapped and placed on paper, plastic or ceramic plates, I walked to the centre of the clearing and intoned my ode[205] as best I could above the ghastly sounds of mass consumption.

'Well done, Anton,' said Chummy upon my return to the log. 'Didn't really get the bit about nuns in water meadows, though.'

'Poetic licence,' I replied.

'Aah,' he said, gulping back the bright pink liquor.

'Well, I thought it was very good,' said Gray, sipping his apple brandy judiciously. 'The reference to Isleworth Bulls will not have

---

202   Unlike the Architypographer, he is a *real* printer.
203   And the female of the species (correctly known as doñas, never madonnas) which we are told are more deadly than the male.
204   The secret of raspberry wine, as many readers will know, is not to strain off the seeds until the must has been fermenting for between three days and a week. The wine should be clarified with eggshells.
205   To be published in the appropriate place at a later date.

endeared you to Vortimer, but who cares? He can't even give you a parking ticket.[206] I note, also, that you do not share Roger Ascham's (and Milton's) prejudice against rhyming.'[207]

I sat down, relieved that the ordeal was almost over. I would still have to recite Robert Southey's famous ode on the same subject, composed when he was Poetry Master (in absentia) in 1801, but *that* was a less demanding task.

Gray, knowing my tastes, passed me a sourdough bap[208] the size of a discus, filled with smoked venison and grated horseradish, lettuce, tomatoes, red onion and cornichons. 'You need to keep your strength up,' he said.

Beetleson chawed at a chicken leg while Gray ate matjes herring with potato salad. The bap might have defeated me without a pint or two of Isleworth Bitter. Even the nineteen-thirties advertising slogan, 'What makes Isleworth Bitter? Thames water,' didn't put me off, but I knew I didn't dare drink more than two pints until I had recited Southey's 'Ode to St Bride'. As a result, I was probably more observant than most of my companions, although I noticed nothing of significance. I hoped that a few would still be awake for my recital. I read and repeated the ode and found I was still stumbling over some of the lines as I muttered them to myself – the great misfortune of dyslexia.

Just when it seemed that no-one could eat or drink another thing, tea was served. Chummy had strong, black Russian tea from

---

206 True – there are no cars within the campus. Isleworth University, like the isle of Sark, has banned the internal combustion engine except for use in agricultural vehicles.

207 Ascham, in *The Scholemaster* (1570), said that 'to follow rather the Gothes in Rhyming, than the Greekes in trew versifying, were even to eate akornes with swine, when we may freely eate wheate bread amonges men.' Milton, while sometimes succumbing to the lure of rhyme, shared a similar prejudice. I would never entrust the education of any child of mine to a man who despises rhyme. I wonder, also how much Ascham knew about Gothic poetry. Indeed, little survives of literature in the Gothic language other than the Bible translations commissioned by Bishop Wulfila.

208 Strictly speaking, I think it was far too large to be called a bap. It was, rather, what used to be denominated an oven cake in Leeds and its environs. These admirable breads are more correctly called oven-bottom cakes, for they are baked in the lower, cooler part of the oven, where they spread laterally rather than rise. In this respect, and this respect alone, they are akin to continental hearth breads such as fougasse and focaccia.

[147]

the St Bridget's samovar with a slice of Barbary cake, rich with eggs, butter, treacle, star anise, caraway and fennel seeds, ginger, currants, candied orange peel, ground almonds and black cardamoms. Gray and I eschewed the cake. He drank his favourite Assam with the merest dab of milk and I sipped a mug of the most delicate jasmine tea. Many of the party, especially the older dons, partook of the traditional cakes and ale,[209] the latter being a sweeter brew than normal to overcome the richness of the cake.

Isleworth, of course, has no cicadas, but the native crickets at our feet did their best to entertain us, as did the birds in the surrounding trees. On the whole, though, it was quiet enough to catch the sound of grey squirrels scampering up trunks and along branches. I thought I saw a wren sizing me up from a clump of wood sorrel. I began to feel drowsy but still had Southey's ode to recite.

Eventually, the band, recovering from their long and liquid lunch, played a short serenade which was my cue. As all students of English literature will know, it is a short poem, but reading it out loud presents problems; it is very difficult to balance the metrical integrity of the piece with the poet's clever *enjambement* which maintains its relationship to the ebb and flow of the vulgar tongue. It was, I suspect, meant to be read with the eyes rather than the lips. Nonetheless, I think made a decent fist of it, even if few of the potential audience were awake to witness it. I returned to the log where both my companions were looking a little the worse for wear.

Although it was high summer, the light was already fading as the sun sank behind the tall trees. After a few more pieces of Handel, the band handed over to a group of Indian musicians who performed a haunting evening raga on sitar and surbahar. To my surprise, this revived the people around me somewhat and I could see the odd person flitting from group to group with more drinks and sweetmeats.

209 After all, there had been no tea available in England for most of the University's existence and tea-drinking is still seen as something of a modern fad by the Isleworth cognoscenti. Before you ask, I have no reason to think that ginger was no longer 'hot i' the mouth' for any of the participants.

'I've invented a new cocktail,' proclaimed the Snakenborg Professor, pouring four parts of pink Champagne onto one part apple brandy and adding a sprig of tarragon.

'Take it easy, Tiger,' advised Chummy Beetleson, 'Or you'll have a thumping hangover tomorrow.'

'You know, you're looking rather fat,' Gray replied unpleasantly.

My duties over and feeling rather uncomfortable from the large, half-masticated oven cake inside me, I started sipping middling quantities of Brentford Extra Stout (known to locals as Brent Crude) and the Isleworth University Press's own brew called Isleworth Long Primer.[210] Also a beer of uncertain origin called Honey-Me-Ducks. I wasn't drunk but things seemed to spin around a bit, or perhaps I was merely sensing celestial motion. Gerrish sipped his new cocktail and Chummy read some poems by Hāfez in the Persian tongue. Quite a linguist, Chummy, which was what made him invaluable as the University's international troubleshooter.

Eventually the volume of assorted beers made itself felt and I wandered off in search of a suitably remote location wherein to relieve myself. The woods were fairly dark and having found an appropriately deserted spot miles from anywhere I found that I was also lost. At one point I stumbled over what I was convinced was the lost temple of Mithras described in Camden's *Britannia* (but which subsequent investigations in daylight proved to be a pillbox built in the long summer of 1939 by some enterprising members of the Local Defence Volunteers). After some more stumbling around and a few grazes from roses, briars and a close encounter with a holly tree, I followed the gentle murmur of conversation (the Indian musicians having decamped to Hounslow), re-entering the clearing on the opposite side to our log. A few people were drinking, a few were talking, but most seemed to be dozing. Over by our log, I could just make out a white, bearded figure coming out of the woods. The atmosphere of the place must have got to me because

---

210   This is apparently a printer's term and primer is pronounced like the comparative of prim rather than rhyming with rhymer.

he looked just like a Druid. He seemed to glide over to Gerrish and I thought he pushed something into his mouth, and then, almost instantly, he disappeared back into the darkness. I walked, a little unsteadily, back to the log. Both of my companions were dozing. I looked at Gray and there was a dark red smear around his mouth. Blood? It was hard to tell in this light.

'Are you alright?' I asked but there was no response. I shook him gently but it made no difference.

By this time Beetleson was waking up. 'What is it, old boy?'

I told him and he delivered a vigorous slap to Gray's cheek with equally little response. Soon there was a general commotion. It was clear that the Snakenborg Professor was seriously unwell. I was just phoning 999 when the Architypographer stumbled over.

'It's Millicent,' he said, 'She seems to be unconscious.' I passed the information on to the dispatcher. Unfortunately there was nowhere for an air ambulance to land, so they would send two ambulances to the nearest road and we would have to carry Millicent and Gerrish to meet them.

We were warned that it might be an outbreak of food poisoning and we should look out for other cases but there were none. Chummy and I used a sun lounger as an awkward sort of stretcher while Behr and some of the other guests carried Millicent. We made our way as quickly as we could towards the road but it was slow going and hard work.

'And he said *I*'d put on weight,' puffed Beetleson.

'This is bad, de Moresco,' said Mitchelberger who had decided to tag along but did not help. 'Where is the ambulance? Where are the paramedics? So much for your National Health Service.'

I didn't bother to reply. It was hard to imagine what American ingenuity or market forces could have contributed to improve response times.

Gray was breathing shallowly and looked half-dead. I hoped we'd get him help in time. I saw the flashing lights of the first ambulance and the ambulance crew ran into the woods, relieving us of Professor Gray. Chummy went with them while I turned back to see if I could help with Millicent Behr. The second ambulance arrived and soon took off with Millicent and her husband. I headed back, meeting various people who were wandering about looking confused. No-one knew what had happened.

When I eventually got to the Isleworth University Hospital, they told me only that Gerrish was 'stable'. Chummy Beetleson, who was milling around, told me that Millicent was dead. No-one knew the cause. In the end we both went home, feeling that it was rather unseemly to hang around the hospital in an inebriated state. Besides, I hate the smell of disinfectant.

33: Black Isleworth – Fifty Shades of Gray

KEENS'S IMPERIAL (Keens). (Syn. Imperial, Black Imperial, Large Imperial Black, Black Pine, Black Isleworth Pine, Keens's Black, Keens's Large Fruited, Keens's Black Pine.) Raised in England from a seed of a large white Chili, about 1806. Probably an excellent berry for those days, and widely disseminated, as is shown by its numerous synonyms. Large, roundish, blunt point, very dark purplish red next the sun; seeds prominent; flesh not juicy, firm, coarse, and hollow; flavor tolerably good; formerly prized as a supposed antidote to asterion poisoning. Tender.[211]

In the strawberry season, hundreds of women are employed to carry the delicate fruit to market on their heads and their industry in performing this task is as wonderful as the remuneration is unworthy of the opulent classes who derive enjoyment from their labour. They consist, for the most part, of Shropshire and Welsh girls, who walk to London at this season in droves, to perform this drudgery, just as the Irish peasantry coming to assist in the hay and corn harvests. We learn that these women carry upon their heads baskets of strawberries or raspberries weighing from forty to fifty pounds, and make two turns in the day, from Isleworth to market, a distance of thirteen miles

---

211 J. M. Merrick Jr, *The Strawberry and Its Culture: with a Descriptive Catalogue of All Known Varieties*, Boston: J. E. Tilton and Company, 1870.

The author, like many before him, is being grossly unfair to the Black Isleworth Pine Strawberry. When grown in the right soil and under the right climatic conditions, as prevail in its native Isleworth, the flesh is so deep a purple as to be almost black, the abundant juice leaving stains on hands and clothes which could be mistaken for those from mulberries. The flesh, when fully ripe, is firm but juicy. Moreover, the taste is quite remarkable, combining the best traditional strawberry flavour with a hint of blackberry. The berries are large, though seldom as large as those of its ancestor, *Fragaria chiloensis*. Its abundant foliage is prized by Isleworth gardeners for the ample protection it affords frogs, toads and newts from the harsh noonday sun, though these creatures seldom, if ever, consume the fruit.

The presence of large quantities of octanoic acid in the fruit is believed to be responsible for counteracting the effects of asterizine poisoning. Similar properties have been attributed to the small black wild strawberry, *Fragaria negra,* which can still occasionally be found in gardens and hedgerows in Isleworth, Brentford, Kew and Richmond upon Thames. Reported sightings as far away as Gunnersbury, Kingston, Putney and Mortlake may still prove to be accurate.

each way; three turns from Brentford, a distance of nine miles; and four turns from Hammersmith, a distance of six miles. For the most part they find some conveyance back; but even then these industrious creatures carry loads from twenty-four to thirty miles a-day.[212]

IT WAS NOT until the next morning, at seven, that we were allowed to see Professor Gray. Chummy and I went together and were pleasantly surprised to find him sitting up in bed eating a boiled egg with soldiers while reading the obituaries section of *The Times*. You can always tell that someone is on the mend when he or she takes pleasure in the biographies of the recently departed.

'It's good to see you *ab ovo* rather than *in media res*,' I said.

Rather than bringing the house down, this simply prompted a brief 'pah!' from Gray, and, looking at him, I realised that his was not a healthy complexion – not pink or even white but somewhere between battleship grey and eau-de-nil and mottled in various shades thereof.

'That nincompoop Williams has arrested Merlin,' Gray said sourly, 'For the murder of Millicent and attempted murder of me.'

'That's absurd,' I said, 'He's still in hospital.'

'Quite absurd,' said Chummy.

'He *is* in hospital, but apparently he popped out yesterday evening.'

'You don't think...' Chummy said.

'Of course not. He's quite incapable. I can't think what he was doing up, though. He's quite ill, you know.'

'How about you?' Chummy asked.

'I'm fine,' Gray replied, 'Just a bit tired. I think I must have had a bit too much cider brandy.'

'*Merlin's* cider brandy,' I pointed out. 'And you were in a coma when they brought you in.'

Gray shrugged: 'They're doing tests, but I feel fine. Really.'

---

212   *North Wales Chronicle*, 7 August 1828.

At this moment, the hospital chaplain, Nsolo Mjeri, popped in. He was a small, smiling man with glasses and skin as black as Gray's was now grey.

'How are you doing, Gerrish?' he asked.

'Fine, thanks, Nsolo,' the don replied, and introduced us perfunctorily. 'How's Merlin?'

The chaplain shook his head sadly, 'He's very tired but perhaps it's just as well or he'd notice that they've handcuffed him to the bed.'

We were all aghast at this.

'Oh, and he gave me this note,' Mjeri added, passing a tatty sheet of ruled notepaper to the recumbent don.

'Ah!' cried Gray, 'It's all clear now. Gather in the clans, Chummy. We'll need a larger room. Now, get Merlin, Big Dave, Teddy Behr, Vortimer Williams, Arundhati, Tim Hutchisson, Esther Dalhousie, Marietta Snakenborg, Charlton Mitchelberger. Not forgetting, of course, Chief Inspector Clanarsh of Scotland Yard – you'll find his card in my wallet, Chummy. And yourselves, of course.'

'What time?' Chummy asked, jotting down the names feverishly.

Gray consulted his watch, an ancient Timex: 'Let's say midday. That should give everybody time and I'm sure they'll all want to come, even if one or two have rather thick heads today. If they don't care to come, it's just too bad. Now, get off, you two. The Reverend Mjeri and I will arrange the room and some refreshments.'

Professor Gray Begins His Grand Oration

So it was that everyone on Gray's list was gathered in the small lecture theatre on the third floor, along with Dr Marleswain and a motley crew of Isleworth Bulls who milled around uneasily, occasionally tapping their truncheons. Merlin was handcuffed to a gurney surrounded by a full panoply of drips and monitors, Gray sat in a wheelchair and the rest of us were ambulatory, although Dr Behr looked very grim, as any man who has just lost his wife might – and should. Vortimer Williams looked sourly at Clanarsh who, for once, was not dressed in tweed but a dark suit and silk tie. It is my understanding that, in the world of crime-fighting, to let a criminal escape is unfortunate but to trespass on another officer's jurisdiction is unforgivable. However, given that one former H. M. Chief Inspector of Constabulary had described the Isleworth Bulls as 'institutionally stupid,' my sympathies were with Clanarsh.

'Now, before we begin,' said Gray from his wheelchair next to the rostrum, a microphone angled down to him, 'Grab a drink and something to eat and sit down. I think I'm now in a position to clear up nearly everything.'

The Proctor muttered something unintelligible and probably unrepeatable. I suspected that it was only Dr Behr's presence which stopped him from dispersing the gathering with a show of force. Neither tear gas nor water cannon seemed practical in this restricted space and, to its eternal shame, the Isleworth University Constabulary has no mounted division – which, in any case, could not have been deployed in the middle of the hospital. They did, however, carry Tasers as well as their robust and gaily-decorated Victorian wooden truncheons. Fourteen inches long and manufactured from local hornbeam, they are exceptionally hard and unyielding. It was entirely possible, although I didn't intend to find out, that fifty thousand volts from the former would be rather less unpleasant than a light tap from the latter. Hornbeam is not a timber to pick a fight with.

'Right,' said the Snakenborg professor, 'I'll be quick because some of us,' nodding at Merlin, 'aren't very well. I shall divide this into two parts: first the homicidal side of things and then the artistic matter.' And he immediately launched into the first topic, but he didn't stick rigidly to the proposed structure of his explication, which surprised no-one who knew the Snakenborg Professor well.

'There have been,' Gray began, 'that I know of, three murders and three attempted murders in the University of Isleworth in the last few weeks. All these deaths are, of course, regrettable.'

[155]

Vortimer Williams scowled and several others, including the Vice-Chancellor, looked surprised at the tally. Gray had evidently not got around to telling the Isleworth authorities about the hole in his study window.

'The first murder was the man found in the Snakenborg Gallery. At first neither I nor the police had any idea who he was. He had no documents on him. Presumably his wallet had been stolen. There were some clues – the nutmeg cola, the poison asterizine, the double-black playing card and the appointment with 'M' might seem, to a complete dullard,' he looked briefly at the Proctor, 'to implicate Professor LeMaistre. There was also the fact that the man seemed to be suffering from osteoporosis, rare in men at any age and decidedly unusual in a man of his comparative youth. I am assured that it is not a side-effect of nutmeg cola consumption.'

'So you say,' sneered the Proctor.

'The second murder was poor Mr Yllingstone. I was standing right next to him when he died. He was a harmless man who made a few silly mistakes in his youth (which I'll mention later) and spent the rest of his life suffering for them. There seemed to be several possible reasons for his death: perhaps there was some dark secret about the Madonna which someone was determined to keep hidden; perhaps the infamous Tweezle brothers, alerted by my interest in Yllingstone, had decided to silence him or extract revenge (but for what?); perhaps the murderer had been aiming at me not him. It was a great puzzle, but the third incident seemed to clear that up.'

'When someone took a pot-shot at me in my study – I'm sorry, Teddy, I should have mentioned that before – the shot could have been meant only for me. Chief inspector Clanarsh was in the room but was far away from me on the sofa. So the shot was meant for me, but was it a warning shot or was it meant to kill?'

'What, didn't even your friend from Scotland Yard have any ideas, Professor Gray?' asked Vortimer Williams sourly.

'No, I didn't,' said Clanarsh, who until now we had all assumed to be snoozing; 'It is always unwise to speculate on the basis of insufficient evidence.'

'Once I knew that someone was shooting at me, whether to kill me or to frighten me, I could only conclude that the shot which killed Yllingstone really intended for me. Gun crime in Isleworth, as you know,' he glanced at Vortimer Williams, 'is just about the lowest in the world. As far as I am aware, violent crime within the University campus is rarer still, so the death in the Snakenborg Gallery must surely be connected too. All three deaths might be connected to the Isleworth Madonna, but I'll come to that later. There is also the death of Dr Millicent Behr which I'll also come to later. In the meantime, can you please release, Merlin? He couldn't possibly have shot at me because he was in custody.'

'Get on with it, man,' boomed the Vice-Chancellor and Vortimer Williams reluctantly ordered his men to remove the handcuffs from the Professor Emeritus of Chemistry.

Gray proceeded to discuss the Isleworth Madonna. Despite his insistence on brevity, his natural showmanship, combined with an incomplete mastery of the niceties of art history and of scientific investigation prolonged his presentation past the natural concentration span of some of his audience. What follows is a brief précis of the essential facts.

The Visit to the Courtauld

Gray described with his usual eloquence and concision, the visit to the Courtauld Institute. Their ramble to Syon Lane had not been as short or pleasant as Professor Mitchelberger had been led to believe and he was puffing and sweating by the time they arrived at the station. To his disgust, the electric locomotive which pulled in almost immediately had no cow-catcher – a big mistake in this rural location, he suspected. Their (completely cow-free) journey on Hounslow loop line took them through Brentford, Kew Bridge (where Gray pointed out the almost unrecognisable terminus of the defunct atmospheric railway) and Chiswick (really Grove Park), crossing the Thames at Barnes and on, through less appealing areas to dingy Waterloo. From there, they caught a bus (how Mitchelberger hated public transport – it smacked of communism!). Gray insisted that they sat upstairs at the front, like naughty schoolboys, although Arundhati Datt probably kept them in order as best she could. I was not there. I had better things to do.

The bus passed the iMax cinema and crossed the murky Thames to deposit them at Aldwych, and, cutting down the side of the Indian High Commission, they arrived on the traffic-clogged Strand (with St Clement Danes just to their left) directly opposite the portals of Somerset House, a building which Gray still associated with the Inland Revenue and the Registry of Births, Deaths and Marriages. Both had long since been relocated; the Inland Revenue (now Her Majesty's Revenue and Customs) had been dispersed to the far corners of the realm – the sort of places that no sane man visits, such as Gateshead and Scotland – while Births, Deaths and Marriages found a natural resting place in the National Archives at Kew. Nowadays Somerset House (a dull eighteenth-century building, not at all like the old Tudor palace which had hosted the peace conference between England and Spain in 1604) is a place of gaudy entertainment, even offering ice skating over the Christmas period. On this summer's day it looked merely grimy, like most of London. Gray took meagre comfort from the knowledge that the grime on every surface contained less lead and sulphur than it had in his youth. No doubt in his tender infancy the lead had addled his brain and the sulphur had punched small holes in his lungs. Think what he might have achieved without these pollutants!

The Courtauld Institute itself, which, rather like the University of Isleworth, seems determined to go unobserved by the rest of the world and succeeds admirably in this resolve, is accessed rather inconveniently through a side door on the left side of the entrance arch. The whole Institute is rather jammed into a most inconvenient space, just as the revenue men were in their day. The lintel above the door was rather elegantly engraved 'ROYAL & ANTIQN: SOCIETIES.'[213] Tim Hutchisson entered the combination on a keypad, opened the door and led the way, although Gray, demonstrating once more his enquiring mind, kicked the door first to test its sturdiness. As an art gallery (which is on the other side of the gateway), the Courtauld is rather small and cramped; as an educational establishment and place of research, it is more so. The building is large and sprawling but ill-suited to any serious task. Tim took them down a flight of stairs to a cave-like institutional underworld quite unconducive to art appreciation or even the meanest trogloditic lifestyle. There were a few stray souls milling around this sterile chasm. Could this, wondered Gray, who (given his atheism) was seldom prey to such thoughts, be the anteroom to Hell? On closer inspection, it was simply a basement.

Tim Hutchisson strode to an easel and pulled off a cloth to reveal the Madonna. 'Well, Professors,' he said, 'It's play time.'

'Oh, do get on with it,' said Gray, for which he received a withering glance from Arundhati.

'Quite,' said Mitchelberger. It was a rare moment of accord between those two professors.

'OK,' said Tim. 'Now, I've already discussed the scientific analyses in detail with Professor Gray. Here are print-outs of all the findings. As I emphasised at the beginning, and as Professor LeMaistre is well aware, scientific analysis alone cannot prove authenticity, although it can strongly suggest it. It will, however, very often be able to prove that a painting is a fake. None of the many tests undertaken here or next door at King's College gives any indication that the work is not a genuine Raphael, and that, in itself, encourages us to think it may be genuine. We now turn...'

---

213 The Royal Society is now in Carlton House Terrace, in what was, before the Second World War, the German Embassy; the grave of Leopold von Hoesch's dog, Giro, is still to be seen there, next to the Duke of York Steps which take you down to the Mall. The Society of Antiquaries is in the courtyard of Burlington House (home of the Royal Academy of Arts) in Piccadilly. I mention it because it is right that you should know these things.

'Surely,' interrupted Mitchelberger with a note of sarcasm in his voice, 'The presence of the Eiffel Tower in the painting is not consistent with production in the early *cinquecento*?'

'It's not the Eiffel Tower. It's the Crystal Palace television transmitter,' Gray replied impatiently.

'Yes, I don't think there's any question that it is the Crystal Palace transmitter,' Hutchisson butted in before Mitchelberger could fire off a still more withering comment. 'We'll come to that shortly. Now, there are two other important methods for assessing the genuineness of a piece of art. The first is simple expert opinion of the piece which sometimes goes by the unfortunate term "connoisseurship". This encompasses an appreciation of the conception, composition and execution of the work, in terms of artistic merit, of draftsmanship and brushwork, etc. and of similarity to other accepted works in the canon. All this is naturally subjective but it is the most important test available. I have consulted a total of seven experts in the field, including Professor Lehmann here, Dr Copthorne at the National Gallery, Professor Perugini in Florence and Dr Art Bechtlesmann at the Getty Center in Los Angeles. I have also discussed the painting at length with Isleworth's own Dr David Trentwistle who, you will all know, is recognised internationally as an expert on Raphael.'

This probably came as a surprise to Professors Gray and LeMaistre who had rather liked Trentwistle but assumed he had been appointed (in the age-honoured Isleworth tradition) for his prowess with the rugby ball and pint tankard rather then a knowledge of art.

'Most unusually,' Hutchisson continued, 'The experts have been unanimous. The Isleworth Madonna is genuine.'

'But,' spluttered Mitchelberger, 'The Eiffel... I mean the Crystal Palace thing!'

'I'll come to that in a minute,' said Tim Hutchisson, 'But there is one more thing. Provenance. Dave has found not only the bill of sale issued by the London dealer to Arthur Snakenborg but also all the paperwork provided by that dealer at the time. Mr Snakenborg appears to have been a very cautious man and he would not have parted with four hundred guineas without the most rigorous proof of authenticity. This paperwork proves, beyond reasonable doubt, that the painting sold to him was the 'most exquisite picture by Raphael' which Giorgio Vasari said hung in the cell of the prior of the monastery of Santa Maria degli Angeli in Florence. Given Mr Snakenborg's notorious mistrust of others, the security with which he surrounded both himself and his paintings and the restrictive covenants which he imposed upon his bequest, we can be fairly sure that this same painting was in the Snakenborg Gallery in Isleworth in 1971 when, unfortunately, the roof leaked.'

'Ah!' got out Mitchelberger, but he was allowed to say no more.

'Perhaps more unfortunately, the Madonna was handed over for restoration to a known forger, Tom Keating. I believe that this was done because Mr Yllingstone, distraught by his failure to protect the works in his care, fearful for his job and in debt to a pair of notorious gangsters, wanted to hide everything from the University authorities. Now, you must realise that scientific analysis has improved quite remarkably since 1971 and it is hard to believe that even a great forger working then would have created a fake which would have satisfied all our tests. Moreover, Tom Keating was not, in my opinion, a very good forger (or even a very good restorer). His fake Samuel Palmers are quite pitifully bad and forging a Palmer is far easier than forging a Raphael – take my word for it; I've tried forging both, as an academic exercise, of course. We know from his autobiography that Keating was sometimes required by galleries to add or remove small objects from paintings, notably sheep – which might explain his subsequent forgery of sheep-rich Palmers. He had something of a grudge against the art establishment and liked to leave little anachronisms in his forgeries which would later be discovered to the great embarrassment of those who had authenticated them. Personally, I'd say his forgeries were so poor that the anachronisms were hardly necessary. Given his known habits, it is not entirely surprising that when he was restoring the Madonna he chose to paint a small image of the Crystal Palace television transmitter, an object which seems to have had a special significance for him, in the top right-hand corner. He painted it over a rather indistinct wooden tower and I am glad to report that neither this addition, nor his minor restoration of other parts of the painting seems to have caused any real harm.'

'Hmph!' said Mitchelberger, 'And why would this guy start painting television transmitters rather than sheep?'

'I really couldn't say,' replied Dr Hutchisson, 'Why did Picasso go Cubist? Why did van Gogh start painting sunflowers? It hardly matters. Now, let me test my hypothesis.'

He lifted the heavy panel with apparent ease and placed it carefully on a nearby workbench, beckoning them to gather round. He then picked up a cotton bud and dipped it into a shallow bowl of liquid.'

'As you've probably noticed, we've already removed the nineteenth-century varnish which had turned very yellow. This is conservation fluid, a mild solvent. It won't do any harm to old paint which becomes very tough over the centuries.' He applied the cotton bud gently to the Crystal Palace transmitter. His body stiffened as the whole area of paint seemed to swim, 'Gosh, I hadn't expected that!' he said and then burst out laughing.

'Just kidding,' he explained. 'That was exactly what I expected. It's what Keating called a "time bomb," a device he used in many of his fakes. He commonly painted on top of a thin layer of glycerine. Totally unstable, of course. With his fakes, any attempt at restoration, or simply the passage of time, could cause the painting to disintegrate. With this, of course, it is only the Crystal Palace transmitter which is fake and, as you see, it has simply dissolved.' He wiped away the viscous liquid and it was clear that the painting underneath was unharmed.

Thus ended Professor Gray's description of their visit to the Courtauld.

There was a short hush as Gray slumped back into his wheelchair.

'What matters,' said Marietta, speaking for the first time since they had gathered in the hospital, 'Is that the Madonna, and various other pictures were removed from the gallery. This is in breach of the terms of the Bequest. The collection now belongs to us.'

'Us,' agreed her cousin Esther.

'No, what matters is that the painting is genuine,' Dr Behr replied. 'And you are wrong to suggest that the terms of the Trust have been broken. The gallery was not even completed until 1888, after the University received the Bequest, so it would have been impossible to require that the works were always kept there. Mr Snakenborg's will, codicil and trust documents actually only stipulate that the collection would at all times be in the custody of a curator appointed by the University. The records show that Yllingstone, as was specifically permitted by his own contract of employment, appointed Tom Keating and several members of the staff at Twickenham Studios as temporary curators. Therefore, the painting never left the custody of a curator.'

You could rely on Behr to get every pernickety detail right. It's what Vice-Chancellors are for.

'But what about right now?' Marietta asked, and her cousin nodded encouragement.

'We have the late Mr Yllingstone to thank for that, too,' said Dr Behr. 'In 1969 he drew the trustees' attention to the fact that some pieces in the collection were seriously in need of conservation and suggested that this might be undertaken at the Courtauld. Rather than deputise individual members of the Courtauld staff as curators, it was agreed that all members of the Courtauld staff would automatically be recognised as such. It took about six months of legal to-ing and fro-ing but I am assured that the agreement is watertight. I have a file about nine inches thick, if you are interested.' Judging from their faces, neither Marietta nor Esther felt up to the wading through nine inches of legalese, however little they liked Dr Behr's conclusions.

'But why,' Merlin asked in a rather croaky voice, 'didn't he send the Madonna to the Courtauld for restoration in 1971?'

'I think he was too embarrassed. He felt responsible for the leaking roof and the damage it caused,' said Gray. 'We found nothing in the University archives to indicate that any paintings were damaged by the leaking roof. They were simply said to have been removed while the roof was repaired. And he seems to have paid for the restoration with his own money – or possibly money he borrowed from the Tweezle brothers.'

'Poor man!' exclaimed Dr Behr, echoing my thoughts, and no doubt Gray's.

The Murderer Unmasked

Gray suddenly looked more serious than I had even seen him before, which, admittedly, is not saying very much. 'Now,' he said, 'we come to the more homicidal aspects of the case. First there was the dead body in the Snakenborg Gallery. Who was he? As I mentioned earlier, the unidentified victim had signs of osteoporosis. I vaguely remembered that Merlin had said – I'm sorry about this, but it has to come out –' he said addressing Dr Behr, 'Merlin had mentioned that Millicent had had a fling with someone who was a "cosmologist," a "rocket scientist," or something else space-related. This was very suggestive.'

Professor Behr frowned, Vortimer Williams frowned, Merlin LeMaistre frowned, I may have even frowned myself, but Professor Gray continued unabashed.

'As is well-known, prolonged weightlessness causes a loss of bone density. This man was clearly an astronaut. It only took a quick check with the Isleworth Space Centre[214] to discover that there'd

214 I need hardly say that we don't launch rockets from Isleworth; there are far too many people around to do that safely, not to mention all those planes flying around here. However, we have had a space research centre here since the early 1950s when we worked on Blue Streak with the Rocket Propulsion Establishment at Westcott and later contrib-

been an Italian astronaut over here to give a series of lectures. His name was Rossini and, from his picture in the personnel files, he is undoubtedly the man I came across in the Gallery. And he is clearly the man Millicent had a fling with. Moreover, no-one has seen him in weeks.'

Gray, who was looking rather unwell, gulped some water and continued. 'Next there was the death of poor Yllingstone. There were,' he looked in Clanarsh's direction, 'a number of conflicting theories about this incident. The obvious starting-point was that it was connected with the so-called disappearance of the Isleworth Madonna. Someone – the Tweezle brothers, possibly – or someone else, didn't want me finding out too much about it. But why? When it was believed to be missing, it was possible to hypothesise that the thief might have a motive. Now we know that the genuine painting is here, another motive presented itself – it might have been in someone's interest for the painting to be *thought* to be missing. For instance, this would void the Snakenborg bequest...'

Esther Dalhousie, in a rare show of liveliness, jumped to her feet: 'I hope you are not suggesting–'

'No, no, of course not,' said Gray with an uncharacteristic lack of sincerity, 'although, now you come to mention it, I was rather surprised to find you'd been sniffing around Twickenham Studios and asking about the Madonna. It was also possible that someone had indeed forged the Madonna, left the genuine one in place and sold the fake as the original to some criminal who would keep it hidden away in a bank vault. However, for that to have worked, the painting would have had to be reported missing and, until recently, it had not been.'

'Quite,' said Behr.

'Another possibility was that *I* was the intended victim, not Yllingstone, and the poor man simply got in the way of the bullet. Again, this could have been related to the Madonna, or to something else. And the only "something else" I could think of was the

---

uted to the Royal Aircraft Establishment's Black Arrow programme.

[165]

murder of Signor Rossini, but at the time of the shooting I didn't even know who he was.'

'So it *was* to do with the Madonna,' pronounced our visitor from Virginia.

'I'll get to that in a minute,' said Professor Gray. 'First, could I prevail on someone to get me a stiff drink? Any spirit will do. Perhaps a large tumbler of Highland Park?'

As if by magic, and despite any number of frowning doctors and nurses, Ketan Patel appeared and poured Gray a large glass of dark yellow liquid with the words, 'You'll have to make do with Bushmills single malt, I'm afraid, Professor.'

'That's quite acceptable. Thank you, Ketan.' He took a slug, some of which spilt onto his blue hospital gown. 'Now, where was I? Ah, yes. When Chief Inspector Clanarsh mentioned that the Tweezle brother had criminal links with Hong Kong I wondered if they could have disposed of the painting there. I already knew that the Madonna was genuine and, as I've said, it's hard to sell a fake as the original when no-one thinks it has been stolen, so it seemed unlikely. However, I knew Dr Beetleson was going to Japan, South Korea, Hong Kong, mainland China and Singapore, so it seemed only sensible to ask him to look into the possibility. And it was very lucky that I did. Perhaps you'd like to take up the story, Chummy?'

'Well, there's not much to say with regard to the Madonna,' said Beetleson. 'I asked about, among our large alumni community in HK, and nobody had heared a whisper, other than Professor Mitchelberger's recent "revelations". There is absolutely no indication at that end that there was ever any attempt to sell either the original or a copy. Would you like me to say anything about the other matter?'

'No thank you, Chummy. I'll get to that in due course.' Gray took a slug of Bushmills and gathered his thoughts. 'So let me summarise: the Isleworth Madonna was never stolen; we have no reason to believe that there was ever any plot to sell a copy of it; the painting never left the custodianship of the Gallery; ergo, there was no motive to murder either Yllingstone or me which could be related to the painting.'

Gray paused and then, looking at Esther and Marietta, continued, Except of course... But, no. It did occur to me, I'm afraid, that Miss Snakenborg and Miss Dalhousie would benefit very substantially if it were believed that the terms of the bequest had been broken but I could never believe them guilty of any dishonesty, let alone murder.'

This didn't sound entirely convincing to me and Professor Gray later confessed that he simply believed them too stupid to be serious suspects.

'So,' he continued, 'I think it is safe to say that none of the murders is in any way related to the Isleworth Madonna. Now, before I go any further, I really must have a bath and put on some proper clothes.'

'But...' said the Vice-Chancellor.

'But...' spluttered Vortimer Williams, Clanarsh, and almost everyone else in the room.

'I'm sorry but I must insist. The indignity of feeling dirty and uncomfortable in a hospital gown is interferring with my thought processes. A long, warm bath, a bar of Pear's soap – oh, and one last Bushmills, perhaps, Ketan – and I'll be a right as rain. I suggest we meet back here in a couple of hours – say 3 o'clock.'

And so, the meeting which we had expected to answer all our questions broke up with nothing but the matter of the 'missing' Madonna settled. Gray pointed his wheelchair bathward, Merlin was wheeled off to his room and I headed for a solitary lunch at the Garden of Earthly Delights.

When we reconvened, Gray was, indeed, looking refreshed. He had clearly had a shave and he was wearing standard-issue don-wear for the warmer months – a fresh, light blue shirt without a tie, slightly crumpled cream linen jacket with light grey trousers and some dark tan brogues, scrupulously polished. There was a sparkle in his eyes which had been absent before, or so it seemed to me, but we poets can get rather fanciful at times. He almost seemed to smile but this may have been down to the three or four Bushmills he had consumed, or the two pints of Double Elephant which had accompanied my own frugal luncheon (steak and kidney pudding) at the Garden of Earthly Delights.

There was a low murmur of suppressed excitement although, in the case of the Vice-Chancellor, the Proctor and one or two of the latter's truncheon-twirling henchman, there was also a suggestion of growing irritation. I have long observed that those in administrative roles are far less likely to brook delay than academics, but even Merlin was clearly losing patience and, when Professor Gray stood up to continue his revelations, could be heard to mutter. 'Do get on with it! It's beginning to seem like a shaggy dog story.'

'I'm sorry for the delay,' said the Snakenborg Professor riffling through some notes while sucking on an extra-strong mint. 'To be honest, I wasn't really looking forward to this. I have some very awkward things to say. Murder is a very nasty business.' How true, I thought. This must have been his equivalent of a two-pipe problem because he then paused to put a second mint in his mouth.

'I'm afraid that, until the bath had revived my flagging brain, I had completely misunderstood this case. There is only one clear connection between all the murders and attempted murders in this case, and that common factor is Dr Behr – Dr Millicent Behr, that is.'

There were gasps from many of those present but Professor Gray did not pause.

The astronaut, Rossini, had a brief fling with her and then called it off, as did Professr LeMaistre...'

Merlin looked suitably embarrassed.

Gray continued awkwardly, '... Millicent, er, she, er I'm afraid she tried, er to seduce me, but I'm impervious to that sort of thing.[215]

---

215 I think I suggested before that Professor Gray was occasionally a victim of self-delusion. He certainly would not have been immune to an improbable advance by Dr Datt.

Yllingstone was, I'm afraid, what the Americans call collateral damage. The bullet was meant for me. Professor LeMaistre, of course, had already seen how everything revolved around Millicent.'

'Did I?' asked Merlin, looking genuinely perplexed.

'Of course you did, Merlin. You referred to her as "the daughter of Hippocrates". I couldn't place the reference at once. It was only when the Master of Waterman's, a rather charming lady, mentioned the death of Millicent's boyfriend that I remembered the well-known story of the daughter of Hippocrates in the Bodley version of *Mandeville's Travels,* a rather amusing piece of fictitious Middle English travelogue. The goddess Diana, envious of her beauty, turned the daughter of Hippocrates into "an oryble dragoun". A kiss from a knight would restore her former beauty but when a suiter, a knight from Rhodes, saw her, he was so frightened by her ugliness that he ran away. She persued him and he fell into the sea. You had obviously seen the pattern and, I suppose from misguided gallantry, had kept quiet.'

Merlin looked rather uncomfortable about this but Gray battled on: 'Millicent lost two boyfriends in unusual circumstances while still an undergraduate. One was poisoned, the other fell into the sea. And then there has been this trail of death here. This is not coincidence. It seemed that Millicent took rejection badly.'

The room stirred uneasily and Gray helped himself to another extra-strong mint.

'This... this is most unfortunate,' said the Vice-Chancellor, but Gray ignored him and continued.

'But there was another bit of the puzzle. Something which Dr Beetleson mentioned to me the other day. He discovered quite by chance that Dr Behr – the Vice-Chancellor, that is, not Millicent – had cut short his visit to the far east. He returned before Signor Rossini was killed...'

At this moment there was a scuffle and Dr Behr attempted to leave the room but was subdued by the iron hand of Chief Inspector Clanarsh on his shoulder. He looked harshly at the minions of the Isleworth University Constabulary. 'You can stay where you are. Eusebius Homerton Behr, I am arresting for the murders of Dennis Freeman, Henry Vine and Giovanni Rossini. You do not have to say anything. But it may harm your defence if you do not mention when questioned something which you later rely on in court. Anything you do say may be given in evidence.'

He turned to Vortimer Williams: 'That should do for now. You can argue about jurisdiction for the other cases if you wish, but I'd strongly advise against it.' The Proctor seemed suitably intimidated.

The Great Man Sums Up

When Behr left, accompanied by Clanarsh and two stout constables from the Metropolitan Police, Gray continued with his explanation (Clanarsh having been briefed earlier in excruciating detail).

'Beneath his rather dull exterior, Dr Behr was always a man of the most extreme passions. He met Millicent at Cambridge when they were both members of the Waterman's College Rifle Club. For him, she was always the only one, whereas, as we know, Millicent had a rather roving eye. It is pretty clear that he murdered both Freeman and Vine when they got too close to her. I don't know how Chief Inspector Clanarsh intends to prove it, but I suspect that Dr Behr will admit everything. Now Millicent is dead, he has nothing to live for.'

'But why *is* Millicent dead?' Merlin asked.

'Let me quickly work through things in chronological order. Rossini had an affair with Millicent, so Behr poisoned him with asterizine, probably in his netmeg cola. He obviously thought that death was too good for you, Merlin, so he framed you for Rossini's murder, planting the double-black playing card and using a poison which might well be associated with you – although asterions grow like weeds around here.'

Here Gray paused for another extra-strong mint before continuing: 'He managed to get quite the wrong impression about me, probably from my accidental chance encounter with Millicent while I was out owling. Hence, the unfortunate death of poor Mr Yllingstone. I think he moved his head just before Dr Behr took his shot. Or perhaps Behr wasn't really a very good shot. He managed to miss me again in my study. The techs at the Met have matched the bullet to his rifle, so that should be quite easy to prove. Anyway, he seems to have returned to asterizine poisoning after that.'

'I didn't recognise the symptoms,' said Merlin, 'But I felt so much better after I'd eaten one of those strawberries that it got me thinking. I was aware, of course, that Black Isleworths were said to be a specific against asterizine poisoning. Then, on the evening of the wayzgoose, it suddenly seemed clear...'

'You thought Millicent had poisoned your nutmeg cola and was murdering all the men who had spurned her,' Gray interrupted.

'Yes, I'm afraid I did.'

'And that ghostly, druid-like figure which Anton claimed to have seen was you in your hospital gown.'

'Yes, I was afraid Millicent would try to kill you again at the wayzgoose, with asterizine.'

'So you sneaked out of the hospital with the remaining strawberries, found me in the woods and forced them down my throat, saving my life.'

Merlin nodded. 'Sadly I didn't realise that Millicent was poisoned as well. So Dr Behr murdered his own wife?'

'No,' said Gray; 'I poisoned her. I was a little tipsy and I was so pleased with my new cocktail that I took some for Millicent to try. Lab tests have shown that the apple brandy was spiked with asterizine. I don't even think it was intended for me. I helped myself to a bottle from your cellar. It looks as though it was meant for you.'

It was a sad tale and the crowd soon dispersed in a sombre mood.

'Look,' Merlin said to Gerrish Gray when the three of us were alone, 'I didn't like to say this in public but you are a blithering idiot. I may be old but I wasn't born in the Middle Ages and my subject is Chemistry not Middle English Literature, so why on earth would you think I'd be quoting from *Mandeville's Travels* or any other piece of medieval claptrap? I've never even heard of it. And do you really think I'd have kept quiet if I'd suspected someone of murder? It was a factual statement: Millicent's father was Dr Hippocrates Hughes-Abernathy. I knew him when he was a medic with 42 Commando during the Falklands War. Not a bad chap. Didn't stint with the morphine.'

Epilogue

I T WAS A perfect summer's day, some two weeks after the ways-goose. Both Merlin and Gerrish were fully recovered and were relaxing in Merlin's garden, shaded by Doyenné du Comice pear trees, heavy with slow-ripening fruit. I was there too. It was a blazing day and we were accompanied by the drone of bumblebees in the agapanthus and honeybees in the rosemary. The asterion flowers were dying back as their black fruit began to swell.

'But who sent the anonymous letters?' Merlin asked.

'I really don't know but I suspect Wendell Tallboy,' Gray replied. 'There were Tallboys on the *Mayflower,* they say, which is always a bad sign. Either him or Marietta. She didn't want me to get to the bottom of the Madonna business, possibly.'

I was reflecting that Gray's irrational anti-American streak was rather distasteful and it seems to have shown.[216]

'You look glum, Anton,' Merlin remarked, pouring himself, Professor Gray and me more nutmeg cola.

'It's not that I don't enjoy being McGonagall Professor, Merlin,' I said, 'and you know how grateful I am for your help in getting me the chair, but I've almost finished writing up the *Isleworth Madonna*. It's been great fun and, to be honest, it's a lot easier than writing poetry. Almost everything is.' To which those to two great lions of academia muttered their agreement, although I am not aware of Professor Gray ever penning a single verse.

'You're not going to write any more about Gerrish's exploits, then?' Merlin asked with surprise.

'As I said, it's almost finished.'

Merlin laughed gruffly. 'Finished? It's only just begun.'

And so it proved.

---

216 However I could hardly disagree with the great man on a previous occasion, when he had observed that, 'An American is one who does not know his Ass from his Arse.' Nonetheless, I'd pointed out that this was due to a linguistic rather than any intellectual or moral deficiency.

TYPESET IN THE UNITED KINGDOM

BY TIGER OF THE STRIPE

USING ADOBE GARAMOND PREMIER PRO

& FRY'S ORNAMENTED

❧

ANNALS

OF THE

Moſt Antient

UNIVERSITY

OF

ISLEWORTH

IN THE COUNTY OF MIDDLE-SEX

from the earlieſt times
unto the reign of

His Moſt Excellent Majeſty

KING CHARLES
the second.

and including

A CHARTER

OF

KING CANUTE

written in the 𝕾axon tongue

𝕾pon:

Printed and Sold by *J. G.* at the ſigne of the Bleeding Heart
MDCLXXXIII

www.ingramcontent.com/pod-product-compliance
Lightning Source LLC
Chambersburg PA
CBHW072138170626
46813CB00004BA/1608